The Winter
DUKE

JILLIAN EATON

This is a work of fiction. Names, characters, places and incidents are either the product of the author's imagination or are used fictitiously, and any resemblance to actual persons, living or dead, business establishments, events, or locales is entirely coincidental.

© 2019 by Jillian Eaton
ISBN: 9781793369499

www.jillianeaton.com

FORBIDDEN PASSION
BURNS THE HOTTEST...

"I have nothing to say to you," Cadence said crossly.

Chuckling under his breath, Colebrook sat up. "Poor Miss Fairchild. Ever the brokenhearted damsel in distress. Do you know the best way to get over someone you used to love?" he asked.

Ignore him, Cadence ordered herself. Ignore him and keep walking.

"What is that?" she said with a jaunty toss of her head.

"Kiss someone you don't." His smirking grin fading as he stared at her with eyes that were dark with lust and some other emotion she couldn't quite decipher, he slowly uncoiled his lanky frame and stood up. "Come in and close the door, Cadence."

Cadence wasn't naïve. She knew what would happen if she did as he asked. Just as she knew there were a hundred – no, a thousand – reasons why she shouldn't.

She swallowed.

Hard.

And then she walked into the parlor...and closed the door.

3

PROLOGUE

"WHAT DO YOU MEAN, you cannot marry me?" Miss Cadence Fairchild stared at Lord Benfield open-mouthed and dumbstruck as she felt her stomach drop all the way down to her toes.

It was not a pleasant feeling.

"I apologize," said Lord Benfield, scratching at the back of his neck where a dull flush was slowly creeping up from underneath the collar of his waistcoat. The ruddy color washed out his pale complexion and drew unwanted attention to the extra flesh bulging out from above his cravat. Catching herself staring at his wobbly double chin, Cadence jerked her gaze upwards. Her lip curled.

"I do not want an *apology*." She placed her hands on her hips, gloved fingers digging into the embroidered lace on her skirt. "I want an explanation. Where is this coming from? Yesterday we had a perfectly enjoyable carriage ride through the park. You complimented my dress. *'Lovely as a tulip in the dirt'* if I recall correctly."

Lord Benfield's compliments, like his physique, were in dire need of some improvement.

"Mother fears the match is not suitable," he muttered under his breath, looking at the floor, the wall, the vase on the mantle – anywhere but at his almost bride-to-be.

"Well it's a good thing I am not marrying your mother!" Cadence had never liked Lady Benfield. The older woman always treated her with the same dismissiveness she displayed towards her household staff. She was a waspish old shrew who had her claws sunk so deeply into her son it was a miracle she'd ever allowed him out of nappies.

Cadence had been counting down the days to when she would replace Lady Benfield as the most important woman in Lord Benfield's life. Now it appeared as if she had been counting in vain, but she wasn't about to let her future as an earl's wife go without a fight.

She'd worked *hard* for this, damn it. It wasn't every Season the second daughter of a baron managed to catch the eldest son of a marquess. It had required countless hours listening to Lord Benfield drone on – and on, and on – about his love for antique buttons. Suffering not one, not two, but *three* sprained ankles (the man was a menace in the ballroom). Pretending not to notice how profusely he perspired whenever they were in close quarters. And, last but not least, putting up with his insufferable mother.

"Lord Benfield – Harold – please." Fluttering her long, dark eyelashes, she stepped forward and placed a hand on his forearm. "Surely there is a way we can make this work. Perhaps if I speak to your mother–"

"No," he said hastily. "That – that would not do. She – she has gone on holiday and I do not know when she will return."

"Holiday?" Cadence barely managed not to snort. "Harold, you and I both know your mother would never leave you for more than a day or two."

His brow furrowed. "What is that supposed to mean?"

"It *means*," she said with exasperation, "that I know for a fact she hasn't gone on holiday. What is this really about? Is it your brother? Is he not getting married after all?"

Lord Benfield's younger brother, Percival, had been engaged for the better part of three years. A wedding date had finally been set for the middle of October, but not wanting to overshadow his brother, Lord Benfield had told Cadence they would need to wait until *after* the wedding to announce their betrothment. She'd reluctantly accepted the delay – really, what else could she have done? – but there had always been a small part of her that had been secretly suspicious.

As she gazed at the sweat dripping from Lord Benfield's brow and the blotchy red wave that was slowly working its way across his face, Cadence realized she should have listened to her instincts.

Harold was never going to marry her.

Not if his mother had anything to say about it.

"Percival and Lady Tibbetts will – will be married as planned," he said, pulling at his collar. "Goodness. Is it warm in here, or is it just me?"

Cadence pursed her lips. "It's just you. I suppose this means I am longer invited to the wedding?"

"N-no. Mother said it really wouldn't be proper given the...well, given the circumstances." Removing a monogrammed silk handkerchief from his pocket, Lord Benfield ran it across his forehead. "I really am sorry, Miss Fairchild. We – we can still remain friends if you'd like. I've just received a new button from a private collection in New York that I'd love to–"

"ENOUGH WITH THE BUTTONS!" Cadence hadn't meant to raise her voice. And she certainly hadn't meant to raise it so high that a maid coming down the stairs with a basket full of clean linens jumped a foot in the air and sent the linens sailing over the bannister in a shower of white sheets and pillowcases. But if there was ever a time to shriek loud enough to raise the dead, it was now.

If she had to look at *one* more button...

"You've broken my heart, Harold!" Snatching her hand away from his arm, she drove the heel of her boot into the floor for emphasis. "Snapped it right in half."

"Have I?" he said uncertainly. "Because you look more angry than heartbroken..."

"And why can't I be both?" Cadence asked shrilly. "I am angry *because* I am heartbroken. If you cared for me as much as you cared for your damn buttons, you would understand!"

Lord Benfield stiffened. "I must kindly ask you to leave my buttons out of this."

"*Oh!*" Too incensed to manage more than one syllable, Cadence whirled in a flurry of indignant skirts and headed for the door. Pausing in the threshold, she cast an icy glare over her shoulder. "You'll regret this, Harold. Buttons make poor bedmates. Very poor bedmates indeed."

Chin up, blue eyes glittering, she sailed out of the house...and made it all the way to her carriage before her anger abandoned her and she burst into sobs.

CHAPTER ONE

"WELL, WELL, WELL," drawled Justin Dearborn, sixth Duke of Colebrook, rake extraordinaire, and overall scoundrel, as he sauntered into his private bedchamber after an early morning ride through the brisk countryside. "What do we have here?"

The two women who were sprawled naked on his bed giggled madly. They'd told him their names at his house party the night before, but damned if he could remember in the lucid light of day. All he knew was that he'd tupped the slender brunette on the left and almost tupped the curvy redhead on the right before they had all passed out from excess drink.

"We were waiting for you," the brunette said, drawing herself up on her knees.

"Where have you been?" the redhead pouted.

"Out for a ride, ladies." Kicking off his mud-spattered Hessians, Justin slowly began to unbutton his shirt as he approached the bed. "I was going to take a nap, although now I think I'll go for another ride instead." Grinning wolfishly, he pounced on the brunette who squealed in delight as she was pushed back into a mountain of pillows.

Not wanting to be left out of the fun, the redhead wrapped her arms around his neck and ran her tongue along the shell of his ear. "Let's finish what we started last night," she whispered, stroking her fingers through his golden, windswept hair as the brunette made quick work of his trouser fastenings.

"That's precisely what I had in – *bloody hell!*" Reacting instinctively, Justin threw himself forward and covered both women with his half-naked body as plaster rained down on them from above. When he looked over his shoulder and saw the gaping hole in the middle of the ceiling he cursed again, this time more vehemently.

'A few minor inconveniences. You'll hardly know my men are working' the architect had said when Justin hired him to renovate his ancestral home.

Lost by his grandfather in a card game, Colebrook Manor had sat vacant for the better part of two decades before Justin managed to buy back the deed. Unfortunately, time and neglect had taken its toll on the old girl and she was a withering shadow of the grand estate he vaguely remembered from his childhood. Which was why he'd brought in Mr. Billingsly.

The incompetent sod.

A bit of noise was a minor inconvenience. Having to take afternoon tea in the west wing parlor instead of the front drawing room was a minor inconvenience. Using the servant's entrance was a minor inconvenience.

Having a ceiling collapse mid-orgy?

That was a bloody travesty.

"Are you ladies all right?" Rolling off the bed, he shook off the bits of plaster and horsehair clinging to his skin. Finding his trousers flung over the back of a chair, he yanked them back on, wincing ever-so-slightly when his hands brushed against his pulsing arousal.

Sorry old chap. Better luck next time.

"The ceiling!" Green eyes big as tea saucers, the redhead pointed above his head. "It has a hole in it!"

"An astute observation," he said dryly. "I trust you ladies to see yourselves out. My valet will see to your travel accommodations. Perhaps we can pick up where we left off the next time I am in London?"

"Oh *yes*," the brunette said breathlessly.

"We could always stay here…" Scooting to the edge of the bed, the redhead suggestively walked her fingers up Justin's thigh. "My husband isn't due to return for at least another fortnight." Her hand slid upward to cup his bollocks as a suggestive smile played across her lips. "Just think of all the sins we can commit in that amount of time," she whispered.

Justin stiffened. "You're married?" he said sharply as the fire smoldering in his loins abruptly cooled, leaving him with an aching cock and an unpleasant taste in the back of his mouth. He stepped back, arms folding across his chest as a dark scowl replaced his roguish grin.

"Yes. We both are." The redhead glanced at her companion, who lifted her brows and shrugged. "I – I assumed you knew."

"No, I was under the impression you were widows or otherwise unattached." His eyes narrowed. "I do not sleep with married women."

"Well you did last night," said the redhead.

"Twice," the brunette said coyly, cupping her heavy breasts.

"Gather your things and go home to your husbands." Yanking on his waistcoat and boots, Justin stalked out of his bedchamber without another word. He intercepted his personal valet in the hallway, a middle-aged man with hair that had already gone gray and neatly trimmed sideburns that framed a long, narrow face. The two had known each other for years, which was why his valet sensed at once there was a problem.

"Is something the matter, Your Grace?"

"Yes, Herrington, something bloody well *is* the matter." An amiable sort of fellow, Justin did not lose his temper very often. It was a surly beast, difficult to control and nearly impossible to rein back in once it had been set loose from its cage. Blue eyes flashing, he clenched his jaw and snarled, "I thought I made myself clear when I said married women were not to be put on the invitation list. Under no circumstances, I believe were my exact words."

"You – you made yourself very clear, Your Grace." Herrington cleared his throat. "I am not certain how it came to be that your wishes were not followed out, but I can assure you it will not happen again."

"See that it doesn't," Justin growled. "And while you're at it, make sure the two ladies in my bedchamber find their way out of it before I return."

"Yes, Your Grace. Of course, Your Grace." The valet hesitated. "Is there anything else?"

"Have you seen Billingsly? There's a bloody hole in my ceiling and I'd like to know why."

Relieved to no longer be the sole focus of Justin's anger, Herrington was only too happy to give up the architect. "I believe Mr. Billingsly is in the dining room."

"Excellent," Justin said, flashing his teeth in a grim parody of a smile that sent a shiver down Herrington's spine. In that moment, a snarling wolf would have looked like a mewling pup if compared to the Duke of Colebrook. "I should very much like to have a word with him. Very much indeed."

"YOU CANNOT FIRE *ME*." Spit flew from the corners of Billingsly's mouth as he stared at Justin in outraged astonishment, thick black eyebrows pulled in so tightly above the bridge of his nose it appeared as though an enraged caterpillar had taken up residence in the middle of his forehead.

"Really?" His anger having simmered to a low boil, Justin leaned a hip against the edge of the dining room table and canted his head to the side. "Because I believe that is exactly what I just did. You told me you were the best, Billingsly."

"I *am* the best," the architect retorted, flushed jowls quivering with self-righteous indignation. "Everyone who is anyone will tell you that."

Justin snorted. "Then everyone who is anyone is either pandering or drunk off their arse. I'd put good money on the latter, if I were a betting sort of man. But as I never pander and I am not – at the moment, at least – drunk, I can finally see you for the charlatan that you are. I just wish I'd seen it *before* your incompetence ruined a perfectly good threesome."

"My – my incompetence did *what*?" Billingsly sputtered.

"It's really neither here nor there," Justin said with a flippant wave of his hand. "Suffice it to say, you are no longer employed. Now take your men and your bloody scaffolding that has destroyed my grandmother's garden beds, and kindly sod off."

The caterpillar wiggled furiously. "You're going to regret this, Colebrook. You'll see!"

"That is where you are wrong, old chap." Justin smiled thinly. "I don't regret anything."

Liar, whispered a tiny, frequently ignored voice in the back of his head as Billingsly stormed out of the room. *You regret one thing.*

Yes, he did. But not for the reasons his beleaguered conscience might think.

It was rare that he thought of Jessica. Rarer still that he dwelled on the treacherous bitch for longer than five seconds. But this morning's events had stirred up the past like a heavy rock thrown into muddy waters and the memories were refusing to settle back to the bottom where they belonged.

Jaw taut, he crossed to the window and threw back the heavy drape to watch in stony silence as Billingsly gathered his men. Justin would see to it that all of the workers were paid in full. After all, it wasn't their fault their employer couldn't have built a simple shed if his life depended on it. But he'd be damned if he gave Billingsly another shilling. No one received a second chance from the Duke of Colebrook. A lesson Lady Jessica Stemworth had learned firsthand many years ago.

And to think he'd actually fancied himself in love with her…

It wasn't until Justin glanced down that he noted his fists were clenched so tightly his knuckles had leeched of all color and turned white as bone. Forcibly commanding his body to relax, he slipped on his customary grin as easily as he'd slipped on his trousers when Herrington appeared in the doorway.

"The two *ladies* have left, Your Grace," the valet announced, his enunciation making it clear what he thought of the women's titles.

"Good. Thank you for seeing it handled, Herrington. I apologize if I was a bit forceful before." One bright blue eye closed and opened in a wink that was as well-practiced – and every bit as fake – as his smile. "Having a ceiling fall on one's head tends to put one in a bad mood."

"Perfectly understandable, Your Grace." Herrington's gaze flicked to the window where Billingsly could be seen climbing huffily into a carriage. "I take it the renovations have temporarily stalled?"

"Do you know how to fix a ceiling?" Justin asked hopefully.

"Regrettably I do not, Your Grace."

"Then I suppose renovations have temporarily stalled. How long do you think it will take to find another architect?"

"I am afraid finding one isn't the problem." Herrington clasped his hands behind his back. "Getting them here is."

"You're damned right about that." There were times Justin thoroughly enjoyed being so far removed from the hustle and bustle of town, and other times – like this one – where being a seven day journey by horseback (longer if by coach) was nothing but a bloody nuisance. He rubbed his chin, fingers scraping against the bristle he'd been allowing to grow for the better part of a week.

"Send out word we're in need of an architect. Go to London if need be. I'd go myself, but with the Season having just started I'm in no mood to have my coattails grabbed by overreaching Mamas and their desperate daughters."

The valet's brow creased, a sure sign he wanted to say something but did not know how the duke would react.

"Oh go on," Justin invited with a negligible shrug of his shoulder. "Speak your mind, Herrington. I've already reached my quota of firing employees for the day. You're safe."

"I only wanted to point out that remaining at Colebrook Manor may not be the wisest choice, Your Grace. For anyone," Herrington added with a pointed glance at a scullery maid passing by the door carrying a large silver tray.

"Why the devil not?"

"You *did* just have a ceiling fall on your head."

"Ah, yes. I almost forgot." Justin wasn't ordinarily so obtuse, but the unwanted memories of Jessica had rattled him more than he cared to admit. Running a hand through his hair, he watched as a few flecks of plaster floated lazily to the floor.

Bloody Billingsly. He never should have hired the man, but he'd been in a rush to see the project done and the architect had promised results before the start of the New Year. Apparently he'd yet to learn his lesson: if something appeared too good to be true...it was. Particularly if the some*thing* was actually a some*one*.

"Let's close the old girl up until she's brought up to snuff. No need for anyone to get hurt. Take whatever staff you need to London with you, send the rest to the village on extended holiday. My Christmas present to them. Except for the cook. I'm going to need him."

Herrington frowned. "And what will you do, Your Grace?"

"I am going to stay with our friendly neighbor, the Duke of Wycliffe." A wry smile twisted his lips. "If he doesn't shoot me on sight, he should prove to be an excellent host."

CHAPTER TWO

CADENCE KNEW SHE could not stay in London. She prided herself on being a strong woman – she'd grown up in a household with three sisters, hadn't she? – but the line had to be drawn somewhere, and if she had to endure one more pitying glance or backhanded insult *(darling, I'm so terribly sorry...but did you* really *think you were going to marry an earl?)* she was going to scream...or take one of her father's antique pistols he kept in a long glass case above his bookshelf and shoot one of her so-called 'friends'. Since screaming and shooting were frownable offenses, particularly if committed by a lady, she had no choice. She had to leave.

But where could she go?

The answer presented itself, as answers sometimes do,

in a most serendipitous fashion.

Shortly before Lord Benfield broke off their almost-but-not-quite-engagement, Cadence's eldest sister had departed London for the feral lands of Nottingshire, a small township comprised of forest and swampland that might as well have been in Scotland.

Why had her staid, obedient sister flitted away to the wild countryside with no more than the clothes on her back and her German maid, Elsbeth, for company? Well, as it turned out, the Fairchild's were in a bit of a financial predicament. One that Cadence had attempted to solve by suggesting Hannah marry a duke. After much debate, they'd set their sights on the reclusive Duke of Wycliffe, a disfigured cripple who hadn't left his estate in nearly a decade.

He hadn't been the sisters' first choice. He'd been their *only* choice. And Hannah, much to Cadence's disbelief, had actually gone and done it. She'd married the Duke of Wycliffe and become a duchess, thus solving all of the Fairchild family woes.

Well, *almost* all of their woes.

As it turned out, money couldn't fix a broken heart, although Cadence had done her damnedest to try. She had three new dresses, two parasols, a fur-lined cloak with matching muff...and eyes that still filled with tears whenever she thought of Lord Benfield's rejection.

Much like they were doing now as her carriage rounded the bend and Wycliffe Manor finally came into view after a long, exhausting journey that had done little to quell her despair.

She hadn't told Hannah she was coming. Not because she feared her sister would turn her away – Hannah, sweet soul that she was, wouldn't turn away a beggar let alone her own flesh and blood – but because putting quill to paper and explaining the reason for her visit was tantamount to admitting defeat, which was something she would never do. No matter how defeated she might feel.

The carriage rolled to a stop in front of the manor. Three stories high with two wings extending out on either side, it was old and in need of visible repair in several places, but the trim had been freshly painted, the windows sparkled, and the leaves had been raked from the lawn, giving an overall impression of disheveled tidiness.

Disheveled or not, the ducal estate was a far cry above the Fairchild's small townhouse on the (far) outskirts of Grosvenor Square and Cadence couldn't help but feel a tiny twinge of jealousy as she made her way inside.

She was happy for her sister. Thrilled, truth be told. If anyone deserved to be a duchess, it was Hannah. Why, she'd raised Cadence and the twins – both of whom were set to make their debut this year – every bit as much as their mother had. She was sweet and kind and good. But it was a well-known secret that of all the Fairchild daughters, it was the second eldest who had been expected to make the best match. Yet here Cadence stood, covered in travel dust and rejected by an earl.

An earl with a button fetish.

Announcing herself to the footman at the front door, she swept inside with her chin raised high and managed to keep her hysterics under control...until she saw Hannah's familiar face. With her dark silky hair, tip-tilted blue eyes, and perfect porcelain skin, Cadence had always been considered the prettier of the two sisters, but there was nothing pretty about her swollen eyes or blotchy face as she threw herself into Hannah's bewildered arms.

"He's called off the engagement!" she wailed, wrapping her arms around her sister's neck. The new Duchess of Wycliffe was no bigger than a strand of thistledown – all of the sisters were diminutive in stature – but in that moment she felt as sturdy as a ship's mast in a wild, rolling sea.

"Who has?" Hannah asked, leaning back to study Cadence with wide eyes.

"Who?" Hating herself for crying but unable to stop, Cadence dashed her palms across her wet cheeks. "Who do you think? Lord Benfield! Lord Benfield has called off our engagement!"

"Perhaps it would be best if you sat down. Come, over here." Taking Cadence by the arm, Hannah slowly led her into an adjoining parlor that was sparsely furnished with mismatched chairs and a velvet settee. Guiding Cadence to the settee, Hannah sat down beside her and turned so the two sisters were facing one another. "Now take a deep breath," she said, her calm, practical tone the exact opposite of Cadence's shrill, panicked falsetto, "and tell me what happened. I thought you and Lord Benfield were not yet engaged? How could he call off your engagement?"

Easily, Cadence thought bitterly. *Far too easily.*

"We were practically engaged!" Her bottom lip wobbled. "Everyone knew it was only a matter of time."

Everyone except for me, apparently.

She'd been like a rabbit chasing after a carrot that remained just out of reach no matter how hard or how high she jumped. Then, when she'd finally pinned the buggering vegetable down, it hadn't just been yanked away – it had vanished entirely and she'd been left with nothing but an empty string and the vague pity of a man who liked buttons more than he liked her.

It was embarrassing.

It was humiliating.

It was *hurtful*.

And Cadence, who had never *not* gotten what she wanted, or been genuinely hurt by anything or anyone, was left shaken right down to her core.

"Good," Hannah said firmly. "You are better off without him."

"Better off?" She stared at her sister in disbelief. Of course Hannah wouldn't understand. She'd never cared about High Society or fitting in. She'd never even wanted to get married, let alone married to a *duke*. She would have been perfectly content growing old with a houseful of books and now their positions were completely reversed and Cadence could not think of a worse fate if she tried.

Unless it was growing old with a houseful of cats.

She'd never trusted cats. Far too smart for their own good, and the way they played with their food before they killed it made her shudder. She could just see it now. Her sisters would come for a visit and they'd find her crushed beneath a bookcase that one of her feline companions had knocked over. On purpose, of course, because cats were vindictive creatures that answered to no one.

'Spinster Murdered by Purring Pussy'.

Heavens, what a laugh the *ton* would have with that headline. Then they'd turn the page and she would be forgotten except for once a year when someone would happen to bring up the story of her gruesome death at a party, and everyone would have a good giggle before they changed the subject and she was once more lost to the anonymity of time. Just another baron's daughter who had tried – and failed – to land herself an earl.

"Better off?" she repeated, shaking her head. "I'm ruined, Han! Completely ruined."

No man would want her now that Lord Benfield had set her aside. She might as well have 'Spoiled Goods' printed across her forehead. It would have been far better if she'd never been courted by him at all. Now everyone would think something was wrong with her. Or, worse yet, that she was no longer innocent.

There were two ways a woman of the *ton* could ruin herself.

By sleeping with a man before marriage.

And by people *thinking* she had slept with a man before marriage.

There was no proof, of course. She hadn't even kissed Lord Benfield, let alone slept with him. But the truth would not keep vicious rumors from spreading, and it certainly wouldn't keep her good name from being dragged through the muck.

Hannah frowned. "Oh, I wouldn't say–"

"He might as well have left me at the a-altar." Her voice broke as she thought of how far she'd almost risen…and how very, very far she'd fallen. "I will never love again." Burying her head in her hands, she dissolved in a wretched fit of emotion stirred by self-pity. Hannah started to rub her back in soothing circles, but her hand abruptly stilled when a man's deep baritone growled at them from the doorway.

"What the devil is going on here?" he demanded.

Her entire face burning at having been caught in such an undignified state by whom she could only presume was the duke, Cadence kept her countenance hidden while Hannah sprang to her feet and hurried from the room. She closed the door behind her, and for several minutes there was only the indistinct hum of voices before the door swung back open and Hannah returned.

"I will have a room readied for you," she promised, pressing her lips to Cadence's damp cheek. "You can stay with us for as long as you like. I need to have a quick word with my husband, but I shall return straight away. Will you be all right?"

Cadence managed a jerky nod and Hannah all but bolted from the room, leaving her to wonder if her sister's wedded bliss wasn't quite as blissful as she'd made it out to be in her letters home. Not that it mattered very much one way or the other. If things weren't right, Hannah would soon fix them. That was what she did. She fixed things.

And I ruin them, Cadence thought with a sour twist of

her lips. Leaning back, she draped an arm across her pulsing temple and closed her eyes.

How perfect she'd believed her life to be! How perfect she'd believed *herself* to be. Beautiful, witty Cadence Fairchild. The bell of the ball. The toast of the *ton*. The almost-wife of the Earl of Benfield. She thought she'd held the world in the palm of her hand...until it had been snatched away and replaced with a hard lump of coal.

Sniffling, she opened her eyes and stared blindly at a long, narrow crack in the plaster ceiling. She knew pity was for the weak and wasteful, but wallowing in it *did* make her feel a teensy, tiny bit better. As long as she didn't get too comfortable, surely there was no harm in feeling bad for herself for a little while. A day or two at most, she vowed silently. Then she'd pick herself up, dust herself off, and find a way out of this awful, awkward, terrible mess.

Lord Benfield would *rue* the day he broke their almost-engagement.

She'd make sure of it.

Unless she was devoured by cats first.

CHAPTER THREE

THE DUKE OF WYCLIFFE hadn't exactly welcomed Justin with open arms, but he hadn't killed him either, which Justin took as a sign their relationship was moving in the right direction.

The two dukes had been neighbors for several years. Certainly long enough for one to think that Justin and Wycliffe might occasionally get together for a brandy, or a hunt, or a visit to the local tavern to drink some ale and woo some wenches. Unfortunately, Wycliffe wasn't exactly the wooing type (or the friendly type, or the neighborly type, or any sort of type which might invite a cordial acquaintance) which was why Justin had been amazed to learn the curmudgeonly old bugger had taken a bride.

Of course he'd had to see the chit for himself. Half-expecting a donkey-faced debutante with all the charm and personality of a turnip, his amazement had doubled when he met the delightfully demure Duchess of Wycliffe, a beautiful, intelligent woman who Evan Wycliffe definitely did *not* deserve and was lucky to have. Something that everyone seemed to realize except for him, stubborn bastard that he was.

Still, Justin was hopeful the duke and duchess would find their happily-ever-after. One might think after his ill-fated affair with Jessica that he'd have given up on such fairytale notions as true love and soul mates and happily-ever-after's, but he still believed in love just as much as he ever had. How could he not, after witnessing firsthand how devoted his parents had been to one another?

He simply did not believe in love for *himself*.

If certain people were destined for happily-ever-after, then it made sense others were not. After Jessica he'd firmly ensconced himself in the 'not' category. And he had no intention of switching back.

Idly tying off his cravat as he descended the staircase, Justin paused at the bottom, gaze flicking curiously to the parlor door. He knew Wycliffe Manor was infested with mice – something he'd learned shortly after his arrival when he'd woken to a pair of beady black eyes peering up at him from the middle of his chest (yes, he had screamed like a lady who'd just discovered a vacancy on her dance card and no, he wasn't proud of it) – but the sniffling and snorts coming from the parlor didn't sound like any mouse he'd ever heard before.

His curiosity getting the best of him, he crossed the foyer and entered the parlor without bothering to knock. What he saw had his eyebrows lifting all the way up to his temple.

It was a woman. A rather pretty one, or so he thought. It was difficult to tell with any great degree of certainty whether the tear-streaked face beneath the tangle of dark, frizzy curls was in possession of a bulbous nose or crooked teeth, but the body encased in a dusty maroon traveling habit was becomingly slender with perfectly sized breasts and hips that were just the right width for a man's hands.

Just the right width indeed.

"I say," he drawled as he sauntered into the room. "Do you need a handkerchief? Although at the rate you're going might I suggest a towel. Mayhap two." His gaze lifted to the tears dripping off her chin and his nose wrinkled. Unlike most men, Justin didn't mind a woman crying. There was something beautiful about a single diamond teardrop slowly sliding down a female's cheek in a soft, silken caress. But there was nothing *remotely* beautiful about a snotty nose, swollen eyes, and blotchy cheeks.

Good lord, he hoped the wretched thing wasn't contagious.

He was considering a full retreat when she choked back a sob, dashed her hands across her face, and lurched to her feet.

"I apologize for the intrusion, Your Grace." Dark hair tumbled into her eyes as she performed a quick curtsy. She tucked a thick curl behind her ear as she straightened, revealing a nose that was decidedly not bulbous. "Due to some...unforeseen circumstances, I needed to leave London."

Justin automatically looked down at her belly. "In the family way, are you? I knew it the moment I saw you." *And without a husband*, he thought silently, noting her left ring finger was bare. The poor dear. No wonder she was beside herself. Although if she ever wanted to *get* a husband she really ought to learn how to cry in a way that was much more flattering.

"Don't worry, love. There are plenty of nice villagers who would be happy to raise a squalling brat. I can provide a list if you'd like," he offered, always ready to play the part of gallant knight – when it suited him.

"What? No!" Flattening her hands over her stomach, she stared at him in disbelief. "I'm not – that is to say, I am not *pregnant*," she hissed, a blush overwhelming her cheeks. "And even if I were, I would not let my child be

33

raised by *strangers*."

Justin rolled his eyes. "No need to be so dramatic, love. It is not as if they would *eat* the child. It's a perfectly practical solution to an unfortunate problem. If you are not expecting–"

"I am not."

"–then you have nothing to worry about." His broad shoulders lifted and fell in an easy shrug beneath his impeccably tailored jacket. The woman pursed her lips.

"Do you know where my sister is?" she asked.

Justin blinked. "Why the devil would I know where your sister is?"

The corners of her mouth tucked into a frown, drawing his eye to her bottom lip. And what a bottom lip it was. All plump and pink and begging to be kissed. A mouth like that would taste like sweet cream, honey, and sin. A mouth like that did not belong on a woman with a large nose or crooked teeth or blotchy skin. It was the mouth of a temptress, and as Justin forced himself to look past her tangled hair and red-rimmed eyes and runny nose he found himself tempted.

Very tempted indeed.

"Why *wouldn't* you know?"

He blinked again. "Because I don't know *who* your sister is? Or who you are, for that matter."

But oh, how he wanted to.

He didn't need to know her name. Names were irrelevant and easily forgotten. But he wanted to know the taste of her skin. He wanted to know the scent of her perfume. He wanted to know if she came in silence...or if she screamed.

Eyes glowing with rakish intent, he stepped further into the parlor. Staring longingly at that luscious bottom lip, he reached for a loose tendril dangling down over her shoulder...only to snatch his hand away in surprise when she slapped his wrist.

"Your Grace!" she gasped, all big blue eyes and self-righteous indignation. "You are married to my sister."

"The devil I am." Scowling, he rocked back on his heels. What sort of game was the chit playing? One he wanted no part in, of that he was certain. Jessica had played all sorts of games and only after it was too late had he realized they weren't playing by the same set of rules. He had no interest in repeating the experience, lush bottom lip or no lush bottom lip. "Are you deaf or otherwise mentally impaired? I told you not two seconds ago that I didn't know who the bloody hell your sister was."

"You should get some rest," she said, speaking in the kind tone one might use with a senile pet or a doddering old aunt named Dorothea. "When my uncle becomes confused he often takes a nap and feels much better afterwards." She smiled gently. "He also drinks a special tea, although I cannot recall the ingredients at the moment."

Over the years Justin had been called many things.

Rake.

Rogue.

Bastard.

Scoundrel.

Best lover this side of the Thames.

But no one had *ever* doubted his sanity, let alone a tiny slip of a wench that didn't know who her own sister was married to. Because it *certainly* wasn't him. He may have drank more than he should and the Good Lord knew he'd woken up in his fair share of interesting places without the foggiest notion of how he'd gotten there, but if there was one thing he'd never done – or would ever do – it was take a bride.

"I am not confused," he said between gritted teeth. "And I do not need a bloody nap or any of your damned witchcraft tea, for that matter!"

Her eyes flashed. "It's not witchcraft tea. And you should not use such vulgar language in the presence of a lady!"

A lady?

Ha!

"When I see one I'll be sure to keep that in mind," he

sneered, his charming façade crumbling away to reveal a rare glimpse at the *real* Duke of Colebrook in all of his varying shades of gray.

Not a prince or a pauper. Not a sinner or a saint. Not a beacon of hope or a harbinger of misery.

Justin had as many layers as scales on a trout, although he preferred to be known only for his handsomeness and dry wit. When someone did not expect much out of you then you did not have to give much in return.

Superficial emotions. Faux smiles. Excellent fashion. That was all anyone expected of the Duke of Colebrook because that was all he *wanted* them to expect.

He'd learned his lesson, hadn't he? He'd made himself vulnerable once. He'd opened himself up. He'd exposed his true heart. And a vicious bitch with red hair and green eyes had gleefully torn it to shreds.

But if there was one good thing about having his heart ripped into a hundred pieces it was that, just like any other muscle, it had eventually healed itself. Except it was no longer the same naïve organ it had once been. Oh no. It had come back hard, and it had come back cynical, and if there was a weak spot in the pulsing flesh and tissue he didn't know where it was. Which why he was so surprised to discover the crying woman had managed to slip under his skin with all the precision of a skilled surgeon. Just as he'd slipped under hers.

"Oh!" she gasped. "You are the most wretched, appalling, *arrogant*–"

"Finally, a woman who sees you for who you truly are." The Duke of Wycliffe smirked at Justin as he entered the parlor, his slight limp only noticeable to those who knew to look for it.

A tall, lean man who occasionally tended toward gauntness, the duke had bold features cut from stone and a defining scar that ran from his right ear all the way down to his chin. He'd gotten the scar – and the limp – in a riding accident when he was only a lad.

The woman's gaze flicked to Wycliffe, lingered for half a beat too long on the knotted tissue embedded in his jaw, and then flew accusingly to Justin. "You're not the Duke of Wycliffe."

Justin shuddered. "Bloody hell, I should hope not."

"Miss Fairchild, might I introduce you to my temporary houseguest, the Duke of *Colebrook*. He is staying here while his estate undergoes renovations. Miss Cadence Fairchild is my wife's sister, visiting us from London." As Wycliffe introduced Cadence, his stare never wavered from Justin. The message in those cold black eyes was unmistakable. *She isn't for you, so bugger off.*

Well that explained the confusion. Now that he knew Cadence and Hannah were sisters, Justin could see a vague resemblance between the two women. They were both beautiful, albeit in very different ways. The Duchess of Wycliffe had a wholesome beauty. The sort that brought to mind warm pies in the middle of winter and song birds welcoming the dawn.

Cadence was the dawn.

Even wet and bedraggled, there was no hiding her exotic allure. It shone through in the tilted corners of her piercing blue eyes and high cheekbones and full, sensual lips. Full, sensual lips Justin had no intention of leaving unexplored, Wycliffe's silent warning be damned.

He'd been wondering what the hell he was going to do with his time. A man could only sleep and drink so much. Now the answer had presented itself in a most delightful way and he had every intention of rising to the challenge. Figuratively *and* literally speaking, of course. It had been a long time since he'd met a woman who had resisted his charms. A long time since one had looked at him with as much revulsion in her gaze as Cadence. The challenge of winning her favor was both exciting and daunting; precisely the sort of thing he needed to get him through the long winter months.

"I would say it is a pleasure to make your acquaintance, Your Grace," she said with an icy toss of her head. "But my mother always told me it was impolite to tell a lie."

Wycliffe's mouth twitched in a rare smile. "Allow me to show you to your rooms, Miss Fairchild."

Justin waited a beat before following them out into the hall. He watched the teasing swish of Miss Fairchild's bustle as she climbed the curving staircase, and when she paused at the top to glance back down he met her gaze without blinking.

For an instant their eyes locked. What should have been nothing more than a flirtatious exchange quickly turned into something more, for in that moment Justin felt an unwelcome and unfamiliar pang deep inside of his chest, as if a screw had suddenly been loosened. A screw that was holding something very important. Something that he could not, under any circumstances, allow to be set free.

So he did what he did best. He shoved his feelings back down into the battered little box where he'd learned to keep them. Then he grinned, and he winked, and he bowed. And when he straightened and Cadence was still staring at him he brought his fingers to his lips and blew her a kiss. Wycliffe murmured something in her ear and they walked away down the hall leaving Justin staring after them…his grin slowly fading from his lips.

CHAPTER FOUR

AFTER SOAKING IN A warm bath and washing the grime from her skin, Cadence felt marginally better. Her mood improved further when she slipped into a clean gown of cerulean blue overlaid with Chantilly lace, and it took yet another turn for the better when Hannah's maid fashioned her long hair into a high coiffure that left her nape and the top of her shoulders exposed. A pair of pearl earrings, a matching necklace, and she almost – almost – felt like her old self again.

Cadence knew appearances weren't everything, but there was something to be said for looking your best. And she'd be lying if she said there wasn't a part of her that didn't want to make the Duke of Colebrook's jaw drop.

Just a little, she told herself as she studied her reflection in the looking glass hanging beside her bed.

Just to get that smug smirk off his face.

How appallingly arrogant he'd been! Yes, the mistaken identity had been her fault, but he hadn't needed to be such a beast about it. She'd only been trying to help. How was she supposed to know he'd been telling the truth when he said he didn't know Hannah? It wasn't as if he'd had the common courtesy to introduce himself. If he had, she never would have suggested the tea. Admittedly not her finest moment, but he deserved at least half the blame.

More than half, if she was being fair.

"What do you know about the Duke of Colebrook?" she asked her sister on their way to the dining room. Outside the manor darkness had already fallen, a grim reminder that winter would soon be upon them.

"Colebrook?" Hannah's head tilted thoughtfully to the side. She'd dressed for dinner in a plain muslin gown with brown striping, her auburn hair plaited in a simple coil at the back of her neck. "We were only introduced recently. He owns the estate that borders this one. It's currently undergoing renovations, which is why–"

"He's here." Cadence's mouth thinned. "Yes, I heard as much. Do you know how long he will be staying?"

"I couldn't say, although I do not imagine very much work will get done once the ground has frozen. Why?" Given her intuitive nature, it was no surprise that Hannah immediately sensed something was amiss. "Has he done something untoward? Colebrook *is* a bit of a rogue. Although I really wouldn't worry. He's perfectly harmless."

"A bit of a rogue?" Cadence said with an uncharacteristic snort. "He could have written the book on them."

And there is absolutely nothing harmless about him.

She thought of how boldly he'd reached for her hair, as if his hand had belonged there. As if he had every right to touch her. As if he had been *born* to touch her. And the part of her that wanted to make his jaw drop couldn't help but wonder what might have happened if she'd let him.

"I take it your first impression was not a favorable one," said Hannah.

"You could say that," she said dryly.

"Well, fortunately Wycliffe Manor is very large and my husband has banished Colebrook to the third floor." Hannah's brow creased. "For some reason he doesn't like him very much."

"He and I both," Cadence muttered under her breath. Her sister shrugged.

"He has always been very kind to me. Either way, aside from a few dinners here and there, you shouldn't have to see him."

"Good," Cadence said with an emphatic nod. "Because I don't want to."

"That solves that, then." Hannah's gaze softened. "How are you feeling?"

"I believe I just made my feelings on Colebrook very clear. I think he is arrogant, entitled, and conceited. Not to mention–"

"I meant how are you feeling about Lord *Benfield*?" Hannah interrupted, looking at her oddly.

"Oh." Truth be told Cadence hadn't given her almost-but-not-quite fiancé a second thought since her little tête-à-tête with Colebrook in the parlor. "I feel sad, of course. And disappointed." Her mouth twisted in a wry grin. "And foolish for having wasted money on silk handkerchiefs with LCB stitched in the corner."

"Well, I for one feel relieved. I know you fancied yourself in love with the earl, but I always found him to be…"

"Dreadfully dull?" Cadence suggested. "It's all right," she said when a flicker of guilt passed over her sister's countenance. "I know you never held him in very high regard. I don't know if I did either, truth be told."

Hannah's brow creased. "Then why–"

"–did I want to marry him?" She chewed on her bottom lip. "For all the usual reasons, I suppose. He was titled, and wealthy, and not unpleasant to look at. He was also kind and thoughtful." *And boring,* a tiny voice interceded. *He was terribly, terribly boring. You know it. I know it. Even his buttons know it.*

"Surely you can find someone to marry for better reasons than those. Or not marry at all, if that's what you want."

Cadence's nose wrinkled. "Not marry? Who wouldn't want to get married?"

"Anyone with a brain in their head." Having snuck up on them from behind with all the stealth of a large jungle cat, Colebrook flashed his teeth in a rakish grin and ran a hand through his hair, sending golden locks tumbling down over his brow. He'd changed his attire from earlier and was now dressed in a black jacket and amber waistcoat. A gold pin accented with a small sapphire held his cravat in place, the deep color bringing out the cobalt in his irises.

"Are you implying my sister is dimwitted?" Cadence said coolly.

Colebrook's smile deepened as his gaze shifted to her and she felt a flush sweep up across her chest when his stare lingered far longer than was appropriate. "There are always exceptions. But I've found those who do not seek marriage are generally the better and wiser for it."

"And what is wrong with wanting to get married?"

"Aside from marriage being an outdated institution

that is worth less than the parchment it's written on?" The duke shrugged. "Absolutely nothing. Marry and be merry, if that is what you want to do. I, for one, have absolutely no interest in tying the knot."

"And why would you?" Cadence asked with sugary sweetness. "When it is so very obvious you're already happily married to yourself."

"Who is ready to eat?" Hannah said brightly. Taking hold of Cadence's arm she all but dragged her into the dining room where Wycliffe was already seated at the head of a long table formally set with lace cloth, ivory China, and crystal glassware. He rose to greet them and then everyone took their seats. To Cadence's annoyance, Colebrook sat down directly beside her, pulling his chair in so close she could feel the heat radiating from his thigh.

His very hard, very *muscular* thigh.

"Are you implying I am arrogant, Miss Fairchild?" he murmured as their first course was replaced with the second, a savory white soup accompanied by a thick crust of bread still warm from the oven.

"There was no implication, Your Grace. You *are* arrogant." Lifting her long-stemmed wine glass, she took a slow, deliberate sip. "I know your type."

"Oh?" Colebrook challenged. "And what type is that, pray tell?"

The type I should have absolutely nothing to do with.

Colebrook may have been a duke (and heaven knew every debutante's dream was to be a duchess) but he wasn't the sort of duke a girl set out to marry. In five or six years, perhaps, when age had curbed his rakish inclinations and he'd stopped staring at everything in a skirt. Until then, a lady of good breeding was asking for trouble just by being in the same room as him.

Let alone living, albeit temporarily, under the same roof.

"You think only of yourself and your own needs." Normally Cadence would never dare insult someone of superior rank – or lower rank, for that matter – but what did she have to lose by speaking her mind? Her reputation was already in tatters. Her good name besmirched. Her prospects nonexistent. If ever there was a time to say what she *really* wanted instead of demurely biting her tongue and batting her lashes, it was now.

"You don't believe in marriage because you don't believe in women."

"Don't I?" Colebrook asked, lifting a brow.

"No. You see us as objects to be used and discarded on a whim. You are a scoundrel through and through, and when you finally take a bride – as much as your type hems and haws and complains, they *always* take a bride – you'll choose her for her obedience and submissiveness, for heaven forbid you marry a woman who sees herself as your equal instead of your underling." Cadence drew a sharp breath. She hadn't meant to say all that. But she couldn't deny the truth of her words, even if some of them had been intended for Lord Benfield.

Cobalt eyes gleaming, Colebrook leaned in close and said huskily, "Your claws are quite sharp, Miss Fairchild. Maybe you can scratch me with them later."

Leaning as far away from him as her chair would allow, Cadence barely managed not to snort. "Thank you, Your Grace."

"For what?"

"For proving my point."

"What are you two discussing?" Hannah asked curiously.

"The weather," she said quickly before taking another sip of wine. "It's colder here than in London. Why do you suppose that is?"

"We're further north." It was the first time Wycliffe had spoken all night. "I wouldn't be surprised if we had snow by the end of the month."

"Then you'd best do something about the drafts, old chap." Colebrook leaned his elbows on the table. "Encountered one the other night that nearly knocked me off my feet."

Wycliffe smiled thinly. "You are welcome to leave

any time you wish."

"Why would I leave when I've finally become friendly with the mice? I'm considering naming one of the squeaky buggers. Right nasty little fellow, but underneath all that bluff I suspect he's soft as a marshmallow." He blinked, all roguish innocence and devilish charm. "What do you think of Evan?"

Cadence's eyes widened.

Hannah nearly spit out her soup.

Wycliffe merely arched a dark brow. "If you've resorted to naming mice to occupy your time, might I suggest a hobby?"

"Funny you should mention that." Colebrook sat back in his chair. With his eyes sparkling with mischief and a grin lurking in the corners of his mouth, he looked like a naughty child that had just stolen the last piece of cake. "I think I've recently found one."

"I'd ask what it was, but that would imply I cared." Wycliffe cut off a small piece of mutton. Their third course, salted mutton drizzled with a sweet sauce and paired with asparagus, had been served during Cadence's impassioned speech. Taking his time, Wycliffe chewed. Swallowed. Set down his knife and fork. "Which we both know I don't."

"Well *I* for one should like to know what your new hobby is." Hannah, ever the peace-maker, smiled encouragingly at Colebrook. "Do tell, Your Grace."

He scratched his jaw. "I believe I am going to take up hunting."

"Hunting?" Hannah's smile fell away. "I admit I've never seen the sport in chasing innocent animals to ground. Especially with winter coming. Will you hunt rabbit or stag?"

"Neither." Beneath the table his hand brushed against Cadence's leg. The touch was so slight that she might have thought she'd imagined it if not for his devious smirk or the way his gaze lingered half a heartbeat too long before it flicked back to Hannah. "I am after much more...*appetizing* prey."

Cadence choked on her wine.

"Are you alright?" Hannah asked, frowning with concern.

"F-fine," she coughed, waving a hand in front of her face. Underneath the table her thighs pressed tightly together as a ribbon of heat unfurled low in her belly. *Wicked,* she thought silently. *The duke was positively wicked.* "P-perfectly fine. Just went down the w-wrong way."

Colebrook nodded gravely. "I hate it when that happens."

"Yes." Eyes watering, she turned her head to glare at him. "I'm sure you do."

"Look, the dessert is here," Hannah announced brightly as two servants walked into the room carrying a large silver tray between them. "Doesn't it look delicious?"

"Indeed," Colebrook agreed, except he wasn't looking at the dessert. "It certainly does."

Cadence waited until he'd lifted his gaze from her breasts. "You know what they say about indulging in too many sweets," she said coolly.

"Really?" he drawled. "What's that?"

Her glittering smile fell short of her eyes. She wasn't afraid of the duke. A bit intimidated perhaps (she'd be foolish not to be), but not afraid. Because she *did* know his type. She'd seen echoes of him on every dance floor in London. Arrogant men all; ones who thought themselves better than everyone else simply because of the title that proceeded their name. Well she was tired of being seen as inferior, and if Colebrook thought to play the wolf to her rabbit he would quickly discover this little bunny's claws weren't just for show.

"It leads to rotten teeth."

His eyes darkened. "I suppose that's a risk I am willing to take."

Blissfully oblivious to the tension vibrating between her two houseguests, Hannah stood up and proceeded to serve the dessert – lemon tarts dusted with powdered sugar – on small porcelain plates edged in gold.

"Enjoy!" she said cheerfully. And if her cheer dimmed and her smile grew tight when she placed a plate down in front of her husband, Cadence seemed to be the only one who noticed.

After dessert everyone retired to their individual chambers. Cadence's bedroom, easily twice the size of the one she shared with Hannah at home, was sparsely decorated with a canopied bed, matching dresser, and a tall armoire filled with cobwebs. She'd meant to ask her sister why the manor appeared as though it hadn't been lived in for the better part of a decade, but now the question would have to wait for tomorrow. After three days of travel and an evening of sparring she could hardly keep her eyes open.

Summoning a maid to help her change into her nightdress, she drew the covers up to her chin and rolled onto her side. Then her other side. Then her belly, and finally her back. For as exhausted as she was, sleep proved to be frustratingly elusive.

When it finally came at half past midnight, her dreams were filled with a blond-haired duke with laughing blue eyes…and the devil's own smile.

CHAPTER FIVE

WHETHER BY ACCIDENT or design – Colebrook was willing to put five shillings on the latter – Cadence managed to avoid him for the better part of a week.

He caught teasing glimpses here and there. Salacious little glances at her trim derriere as she flitted from one room to the next, always one step ahead with nary a minute to spare. Following her sister around like a puppy dog as the Duke and Duchess of Wycliffe prepared to leave on their honeymoon, having finally reconciled their differences after they realized what everyone else already knew: they were head over heels for each other.

Twice he'd caught Cadence by herself aned twice she'd rebuked him, her tongue every bit as sharp as her cheekbones. Their last encounter still made him grin whenever he thought of it. They'd passed each other in the foyer, he on his way out and she on her way in, white snowflakes glistening like diamonds in her dark, silky hair. Dark, silky hair he wanted desperately to touch.

"Excuse me," she'd said bluntly, stepping to his right. He could have easily let her pass, but then what would have been the fun in that? So he'd stepped in front of her and she had tried to go back to the left, but for a man of his stature he was surprisingly quick.

"Can I help you?" A tiny notch marred the smooth skin between her winged eyebrows as she glared up at him. He was tempted to smooth the irritated mark with his thumb, but knowing she was just as likely to snap his hand off at the wrist as allow him to touch her he kept his arms behind his back. He enjoyed Cadence's feistiness, but not at the expense of a limb.

"It looks like it's snowing rather hard." His gaze drifted down to a thick curl she'd tucked behind her ear. It was damp from the snow, as was her fur-lined hat and the shoulders of her wool cloak. There was more snow on the tips of her boots and a single snowflake clung to the tip of her nose. As he watched it slowly melted, proving that Cadence wasn't as cold and frigid as she'd have him believe.

Beneath that frosty exterior was a flesh and blood woman.

One with desire in her eyes and passion in her blood.

What he wouldn't give for a taste of both…

At least now he knew why she wanted nothing to do with him. Or why she pretended she didn't. He'd overheard a conversation between her and her sister, not enough to fill in all the pieces of the puzzle but enough to give him the general idea of its shape.

There'd been a broken engagement. The details remained obscure, but he'd witnessed enough ruined relationships to understand the gist of it and his only opinion on the matter was that any bloke stupid enough to let her go did not deserve her. Once Cadence finally realized the same perhaps she'd stop sulking in her room like a chastised child sent to bed without any supper.

"It *is* snowing. What astute observational skills you possess, Your Grace." Tip-tilted eyes peered mockingly up at him beneath thick, sooty lashes. "Tell me, was it the snow on my shoes or the flecks of white falling from the sky that gave it away?"

Colebrook grinned. No female had ever set him back on his heels quite like Miss Cadence Fairchild. He couldn't remember the last time someone had challenged him as she did. Which was probably why he was so intent on winning her favor. If there was one thing he couldn't stand, it was not getting what he wanted.

And he dearly, dearly wanted Cadence.

To what extent, he couldn't say. He knew he didn't want a wife, and Cadence was not the sort of woman a man tupped and then forgot. She'd make a fine mistress, but he wasn't after stealing her future unless she gave it to him willingly, and why would she do that when she could have any man she desired? Well, any man aside from the Earl of Benfield. The bloody fool.

For now he'd settle for a kiss…although he suspected that once he tasted the sweet nectar of her lips he wouldn't be satisfied until he tasted them again. And again. And again…

"A little bit of both. You've jewels in your hair, you know." Unable to keep his hands to himself even though he risked another slap, he reached out and brushed his knuckles against a silky tendril. Her eyes softened for the briefest of moments before she bared her teeth and jerked her head to the side.

"Have you already started drinking?" she asked suspiciously. "It's not yet noon."

"And when has the time of day ever dictated when a man can and cannot enjoy a nice glass of brandy?" Colebrook wanted to know. "But to answer your question, love, no, I've not had a drop of alcohol since…" He racked his brain. "Last night at dinner."

"You poor thing," Cadence said dryly. "However will you survive?"

Impertinent wench, he thought with no small amount of amusement.

"I am going to meet with a new architect. Would you care to join me? We can take one of Wycliffe's carriages."

"I'd rather attend a ball at Almack's in last Season's gown." Nose in the air, Cadence sailed past him and up the stairs. Justin waited patiently at the bottom, for he knew what would happen when she reached the top. They'd done this dance enough times over the past weeks for him to know every single step.

She would turn and look down at him after she'd crossed the uppermost stair, her plump lips pinched in a scowl that didn't quite match the gleam of interest in those intelligent eyes. Their gazes would meet and hold. Then he would bend at the waist and blow her a kiss, just like he'd done the very first day they met.

Three steps to go…Two steps…One…

Her hair tumbled down her back in a waterfall of rich mahogany silk as she spun around and rested her gloved hands on the bannister. She blushed when he brought his fingers to his lips – she *always* blushed – and then she was gone without a word, back to her rooms where he imagined she spent her afternoons eating chocolate and pining after a man not fit to lick the mud from her shoes.

Justin had come to enjoy their little cloak and dagger

interactions, but he didn't realize just how *much* he enjoyed them until one afternoon when he found himself waiting in the parlor in hopes she'd walk past.

The Duke of Colebrook, waiting for a woman so he might engage in a war of words before blowing her a kiss as she marched away from him. It was nothing short of absolute lunacy. And yet here he was, stretched out on a velvet chaise lounge pretending to read a magazine article detailing the migration habits of gold crested swallows.

How utterly embarrassing. If his mates in London could see him now they'd piss themselves laughing. He hadn't been this distracted by a woman since Jessica, and God himself knew how much of a bloody debacle *that* had been. Thinking about their tumultuous affair all these years later still made the back of his skull ache. It was also a stark reminder of why he only engaged in cheap, meaningless relationships. Ones based on pure, unadulterated passion and nothing else.

No feelings. No emotions. No manipulations.

It was easier that way, he'd discovered. Easier to feel nothing than to feel too much. Easier to languish in pleasure than to drown in pain.

That's all he wanted from Cadence. A bit of pleasure, and then he could forget about her. A little passion, and then he could move on. A harmless kiss or two, and then he could go to London, tup the first comely wench that crossed his path, and forget Miss Cadence Fairchild had ever existed.

Or so he told himself.

"Going back to your room to mope about and eat more chocolate?" he queried when she walked past the parlor. She hesitated, and he could all but see the gears in that clever brain of hers spinning round and round as she tried to decide whether to stop or keep going. To his delight, she stopped.

No feelings, he reminded himself when she peered in the door and frowned at him. *No emotions. No manipulations.*

Oh, but what he wouldn't give for a taste of that plump bottom lip.

"I have nothing to say to you," she said crossly.

If that's true, little lamb, then why are you talking to me?

Chuckling under his breath, Justin sat up and kicked his long legs out in front of him, a mocking grin curling the edges of his mouth. "Poor Miss Fairchild. Ever the brokenhearted damsel in distress. Do you know the best way to get over someone you used to love?"

She regarded him warily. "What is that?"

"Kiss someone you don't." His grin fading as his stomach muscles clenched in anticipation, Justin slowly uncoiled his lanky frame and stood up. "Come in and close the door, Cadence."

It was the first time he'd used her given name. It tasted sweet on his tongue and he wanted to say it again when her eyes were dark with desire. He wanted to whisper it in her ear when she was writhing beneath him. He wanted to growl it against her skin when she clenched hot and tight around him. He wanted, and he yearned, and he waited, breath held deep in his lungs, for her to turn on her heel and flee up the stairs just like she'd done a dozen times before.

But this time was different, because she didn't turn.

She didn't flee.

Instead she walked into the parlor...and closed the door.

I'VE LOST MY MIND, Cadence decided when she heard the click of the door closing behind her. *It's the only thing that makes any sense.*

Because obeying Colebrook's command made about as much sense as a lamb stepping into the lion's den. Which was to say, no sense at all. And yet here she stood, all wide eyes and soft fleece, waiting for the lion to do with her what he willed. No, not waiting. *Wanting* the lion to do with her what he willed.

Wanting was better than waiting. She'd waited for Lord Benfield, and what had that gotten her? Splashed across the front of the gossip pages, that's what. Maybe they hadn't used her name – they never used names – but everyone knew precisely which 'ebony-haired, coyly smiling baron's daughter' Lady Prudence had been referring to in her latest column.

Coyly smiling.

What a bunch of rubbish.

She wasn't coyly smiling now, was she? While she waited for Colebrook to take the next step in the complicated dance they'd begun on the day of her arrival she wasn't smiling *or* frowning. Her lips were flat and relaxed. The corners of her eyes were devoid of crinkles. Her cheeks were neither red nor pale but a pleasing pink that complimented her dark hair. By all outward appearances she was calm and completely collected…save the butterflies that were flying madly around in her belly.

Thankfully, the duke couldn't see those.

"Well I am here and I have closed the door," she said when she couldn't bare the silence any longer. Not with him staring at her with those intense eyes that were the same deep, rich color of her favorite sapphire earrings. "What do you propose we do next?"

Mouth curving, he beckoned her forward with a crook of his finger. "Come here, love, and I'll show you."

The devil himself couldn't have tempted her any more

than Colebrook did. She knew in her head that he was wicked. She knew in her head that he was wrong. She knew in her head that kissing him would lead down a road from which there would be no easy return. But she wasn't listening to her head. For once, she was listening to her heart. And it was telling her if she *didn't* kiss him she would regret it.

For her entire life Cadence had followed the rules. She'd been the perfect daughter, the perfect lady, the perfect almost-fiancée. And what had all of that perfection gotten her?

Nothing.

It had gotten her nothing but a besmirched reputation and an addiction to chocolate. So why *shouldn't* she dance with the devil? If she was already ruined then she might as well do something worth ruining herself for. And who knew? Perhaps wickedness would bring her what perfection had not.

"You surprise me, Miss Fairchild," Colebrook said when she stepped into his arms. He held her lightly, his large hands touching her elbows, the tips of his Hessians brushing against the hem of her dress. His entire body radiated heat, the sort that burned low and intensely hot. She found herself drawn to it – drawn to *him* – as a moth was to a flame, and even though her head knew what happened to the moth when it fluttered too close to the fire her heart didn't care.

Her heart wanted to burn.

Tilting her head back she met his gaze and now she did smile coyly, the corners of her mouth slanting in a smirk that was decidedly feline. "I am pleased to hear it, as I imagine you are not the sort of man who is usually surprised."

"Not nearly enough," he agreed.

"This doesn't change anything, you know." She wet her bottom lip with a sweep of her tongue and watched his gaze darken. "I still find you appallingly arrogant and I do not like you very much." Her shoulders lifted in a small, careless shrug. "Not very much at all, if I am being completely honest."

A tawny eyebrow shot upwards. "I don't know whether to be insulted or elated. A bit of both," Colebrook decided after a thoughtful pause. "Although it does beg the question as to why you came into the parlor and closed the door."

"You said it yourself. The best way to get over someone you used to love is to kiss someone you don't." With the tip of her finger she boldly traced a shiny silver button on his waistcoat. Cadence may have been a virgin, but she was no shy, simpering miss. She enjoyed pleasure in all of its many forms. The brush of silk against her skin, a pair of new shoes, sinking into a warm bath scented with lavender. What was flirting with a handsome duke, if not just another type of pleasure?

A dangerous type, her head warned. *The type you shouldn't have anything to–*

Oh do shut up, her heart interrupted. *Let's get on with the kissing, shall we?*

"So I did," he murmured, and the butterflies in her belly went wild when he tightened his grip and yanked her against his hard chest.

She had one moment to think that maybe kissing a handsome duke renowned for his rakish behavior wasn't such a good idea after all before he lowered his mouth to hers…and then she didn't think of anything at all.

Chapter Six

JUSTIN DID NOT KNOW how many women he'd kissed. Having started at a very young age, he'd lost track of the number years ago. But he did know, beyond an immeasurable doubt, that he'd never kissed one like Miss Cadence Fairchild.

He'd been expecting a little warmth. Instead he got fire.

He'd been expecting a little desire. Instead he got passion.

He'd been expecting a little kiss. Instead he got – well, he didn't know *what* he'd gotten except it sure as the devil wasn't little.

Justin did not kiss Cadence so much as sink into her. He cupped the nape of her neck, fingers tangling in all that dark, silky mane he'd been yearning to touch. His other hand settled on her delicate jaw, thumb resting on the throb of her pulse. Her lips parted and his tongue slid between them. She tasted of cinnamon with a hint of something spicier. Something hotter. Something that wrenched a rumbling growl of pleasure from the depths of his chest.

He felt her pulse quicken as their kiss deepened. As it grew and changed and became more. More than anything he'd ever felt with the women he invited carelessly into his bed. More than anything he'd ever experienced with Jessica whose kisses had always been tentative and teasing in their brevity.

There was nothing tentative about Cadence. She was bold and fearless and she turned his blood to liquid fire. One taste of her lips and he was burning from the inside out. One kiss and he was a man engulfed in flame.

"Well," he said when they finally broke apart, both of them breathing harshly. He glanced at the windows overlooking the front lawn and was mildly surprised to discover the glass wasn't covered in a layer of steam.

"Well," she replied, all flushed cheeks and swollen lips and wide blue eyes.

Justin waited a beat. "Care to do that again?"

"Yes," she said without hesitation. "Oh, yes."

This time their kiss carried them over to the chaise lounge. Cadence gasped when he lifted her effortlessly in his arms and laid her down upon it. Groaned when he knelt on top of her and traced the sensitive outer shell of her ear with his tongue. Whimpered when he cupped her breasts through the soft fabric of her bodice.

He wanted to rip off her gown. Wanted to hear the *ping* of the pearl buttons striking the floor as he exposed those beautiful breasts. Wanted to feel her hands pulling on his hair as he suckled her nipples. But he restrained himself, knowing that now wasn't the time and the parlor wasn't the place. Not when anyone could walk in on them at any moment. When he took her – and he *would* take her – it would be on red silk sheets and a bed as soft as a cloud. They'd have all the time in the world, and he would use that time to explore every single inch of her delectable little body…with his tongue.

"We – we should stop." Pushing against his chest, Cadence rolled out from beneath of him and stumbled to her feet. Her dress was askew, her hair a tumbled mess of dark curls. She looked like a siren that had just risen from the sea, and Justin had the feeling if he wasn't careful he'd soon find himself snared within her net.

"And here I was just getting started." Grinning, he sat up and took a moment to adjust his trousers. His erection was hard and heavy, and when he caught Cadence staring at it his grin widened. "Fancy a trip upstairs, love?"

"No," she said quickly. Too quickly, to Justin's way of

thinking. Her cheeks as red as the Queen's royal cloak, she jerked her gaze away. "Certainly not."

"Certainly not," he mocked lightly. "You weren't telling me 'certainly not' ten seconds ago when my hands were on your–"

She folded her arms across her breasts. "That was a mistake. A temporary lapse in judgement."

"That was a lot of things, sweetheart. But mistake wasn't one of them." Stretching his arms out across the top of the chaise lounge, he tilted his head back and studied her countenance beneath a rakishly arched brow. "Well, did it work?"

"Did what work?"

"The kiss. Did it work or are you still helplessly, hopelessly in love with your earl?"

"I was never–" She cut herself short.

"You were never...what?" Justin coaxed, unconsciously sitting up straighter.

Not that it mattered whether she'd loved her almost-fiancé. She could still be head over heels for all he cared.

Then why do you want to know? A little voice intruded slyly. *You're not jealous, are you?*

Jealous? He snorted at the thought. Jealousy was an emotion strictly reserved for those who cared. Which he didn't. Not even a little bit. He just wanted to know because...because he did. He didn't need a *reason*. And even if he had one, it wouldn't be *jealousy*.

Certainly not.

"Nothing," she snipped. "It is none of your concern."

With the stealthy speed of a lion, Justin sprang off the lounge and intercepted Cadence before she could march out of the parlor. She took a step back and glowered up at him, arms unfolding to rest tersely at her sides, hands curled into small fists.

"What do you want *now*?"

"You didn't love your earl." For the life of him, he didn't know whether he was making a statement or asking a question.

"What part of 'none of your concern' do you not understand?" she demanded, her dark brows sweeping together to form an angry peak above the dainty bridge of her nose.

She was right. It wasn't his concern. Nothing about her was his concern. He should have never stopped her from leaving. Should have never kissed her. Should have never wondered what she would taste like. But he'd done all three of those things, and having done them he couldn't stop himself from saying, "If you loved him you wouldn't have been able to kiss me like that."

Confusion flickered in her cerulean gaze. "Like what?"

"Like this," he said huskily before he cupped her waist

and kissed her again. She resisted for less than a heartbeat, and then her rigidity dissolved like honey melting into warm tea.

This kiss was softer than the last and all the more meaningful for it. They drank each other in by degrees. A lick here. A nibble there. A soft sigh. A whispered moan. And when it was over she stared at him and he stared at her, both recognizing that something significant had just happened between them but neither one willing to admit or acknowledge what it was.

When she bolted out the door in a swirl of wrinkled skirts and tangled black hair he didn't try to stop her. Truth be told he couldn't have even if he'd wanted to. His legs were rooted to the spot, his boots nailed to the floorboards as if they'd been planted there by the bloody gardener.

It was just a kiss, he told himself. *It doesn't mean anything.*

Except it wasn't, and it did. Justin was guilty of many sins, but lying wasn't one of them. Not to others and not to himself. Which meant he knew it was more than a kiss. Bollocks, a *blind* man could have seen it was more than a kiss. How much more, he couldn't say. But he did know one thing with absolute certainty.

This may have been his first kiss with Miss Cadence Fairchild…but it sure as hell wasn't going to be his last.

Chapter Seven

SURELY THERE WERE worse things than being trapped in a house with a notorious rake, Cadence mused several days later as she helped one of the maids hang garland in the drawing room, but at the moment she couldn't think of a single one.

Every time she turned around there was Colebrook, his mouth curved in a wolfish grin as he eyed her up as if she were a tasty little treat he couldn't wait to devour. But that wasn't the worst part. The worst part was she *wanted* to be devoured. And therein laid the problem.

One kiss could easily be attributed to a lapse in judgement. Which it had been. A terrible, *terrible* lapse in judgement. But two kisses? Two kisses were dangerously close to forming a habit, and Cadence had always done her best to avoid poor habits.

She did not chew her fingernails.

She did not eat or drink to excess.

And she did not kiss scoundrels.

Except she had. She *had* kissed a scoundrel, and – heaven help her – she wanted to do it again.

I kissed a rake…and I liked it.

"But you cannot," she said aloud as she stretched up on her tiptoes and draped one end of the garland over the mantle. With two weeks to go until December twenty-fifth and very little to occupy her time aside from her secret stash of chocolate (the *one* bad habit she allowed herself), she'd decided to decorate the manor for Christmas. A fool's errand, given that Hannah and Wycliffe wouldn't be returning until after the New Year and she highly doubted Colebrook would appreciate her efforts. But she needed *something* to distract her from the handsome duke and his sultry stares and, given the time of year, this seemed the most logical choice.

All morning long servants had been dragging pine boughs into Wycliffe Manor by the bucketful. They'd set up an assembly line of sorts in the middle of the foyer and were busy creating large wreaths and long ropes of garland which would be placed on all the mantles and woven down the bannisters. Big red bows had already been hung from the windows and sprigs of holly berries brightened up the sills. The only thing left to do was find and decorate the tree; an old German tradition that had recently been made popular in England by Queen Victoria's German husband, Prince Albert.

"Did you say something?" Elsbeth asked as she stepped down off a wooden stool and brushed pine needles from her apron. Even though the pretty blonde-haired lady's maid was Hannah's companion, she'd stayed behind to serve Cadence.

"I was just talking to myself." Hands on her hips, Cadence took a step back and studied the garland they'd hung with a critical eye. "Do you think the left side is even?"

"Looks good enough to me." Sauntering unannounced into the drawing room, Colebrook stopped directly behind Cadence. Not close enough to touch – he hadn't touched her since their moment of passion in the parlor – but she could still feel him all the same. The heat of his body. The scent of his cologne. The way the air seemed to grow taut with anticipation whenever he stepped into a room. It all combined to twist her stomach into a heavy knot of confused desire.

Unfortunately, while kissing the duke *had* made her forget about Lord What's-His-Name, it had also opened up an entirely new box of problems. There wasn't a doubt in her mind that if she showed even the tiniest inclination

Colebrook would take her to his bed and make her his mistress. But a mistress wasn't the same thing as a wife, and having already been spurned once by a man she'd hoped to marry she had no interest in being rejected a second time. Which was why she couldn't – she *wouldn't* – kiss him again.

No matter how much she wanted to.

"I see you've managed to drag yourself out of bed before noon," she said with a dismissive glance over her shoulder. "Congratulations."

"Couldn't sleep with all the racket going on." Stepping up beside her, he rubbed his jaw where he'd allowed several days' worth of golden scruff to grow. While Cadence ordinarily preferred men who were clean shaven, she had to admit that Colebrook's beard only added to his roguish appeal.

Blast the man, she thought, biting down hard on the inside of her cheek. Why couldn't he be hideously ugly, or dreadfully dull? Maybe then she would be able to ignore him. Maybe then she wouldn't be constantly reminded of what it had felt like to be wrapped in his arms. His mouth on her mouth. His tongue tasting her tongue. His hands – well, best not to think about his hands. Or his fingers. Those clever, clever fingers.

Jerking her gaze back to the mantle as a warm blush blossomed across her cheeks, she silently willed him to go away. When they were in separate wings of the manor she could keep a relatively sensible thought in her head. But when he was standing right next to her…well, all sensibility went right out the nearest window.

"Peterson mentioned you needed a tree," he said, referring to the Duke of Wycliffe's personal valet who, like Elsbeth, had remained behind after the newlyweds made it clear they wanted privacy on their honeymoon.

"Did he?" she murmured noncommittally.

Please go away. Please, please, please.

"Indeed. Coincidentally enough, I know just where to find one."

How was he knew the *one* thing to say that would get her attention? Cadence had sent footmen out far and wide to scour the estate for the perfect Christmas tree, but they'd yet to find one that wasn't too small, or too big, or too scraggly. "You do?" she asked, turning towards him with a raised brow. "Where is it?"

"You can see it from my library. Beauty of a fir tree. She'd look gorgeous right there," he said, pointing to the corner of the room where Cadence had moved the furniture aside to make way for a tree that, until now, have proved impossible to find.

"You don't mind having it cut down?" she asked.

Colebrook shook his head. "Was going to have to do it anyways as she's right in the middle of my future

75

billiards room. At least this way she'll go to good use."

"That's – that's very kind of you." *Uncharacteristically kind*, Cadence thought as her eyes narrowed. "What do you want in return?"

"What do I want?" Adopting an expression of feigned hurt, he spread his arms wide. "Absolutely nothing. Wycliffe has been gracious enough to offer me his hospitality and I would like to return the favor. Although you *do* know they won't be back until after Christmas."

"I intend to keep the decorations up until they return as a welcome home gift. The gardener has assured me if we keep the tree in a basin of water it will not begin to lose its needles for several weeks."

Colebrook snorted. "Trust the Germans to kill something and then keep it alive for months."

Despite her best intentions to remain completely and utterly aloof (her only defense against the duke's considerable charms), Cadence couldn't help but smile. "Indeed. Well then, should I send the footmen to retrieve it? They've a sleigh hitched and ready. Is the library on the east wing or the west?"

"The west," he said. "But you needn't dispatch the footmen. We're going to cut it down."

Her smile faded. "By 'we' surely you do not mean–"

"You and I, sweetheart," he said with a wink.

"Oh, no." At the mere thought of sharing a sleigh with

him – of having their thighs touch beneath a fur lined blanket and their cold breath mingle in the frosty air – the knot in her belly twisted and tightened. "I couldn't possibly. There's so much to do here–"

"I can see that it all gets taken care of," Elsbeth chirped. "You needn't worry about a thing."

No, Cadence thought as she choked back a strangled laugh. *There isn't a single thing to worry about. Except being ravished by a scoundrel in the snow.*

And loving every second of it.

"I am sure the footmen are more than capable of seeing the job done." She folded her hands and lifted her chin, the very picture of a polite, well-behaved lady. Not at all the sort who would indulge in a passionate kiss with a lecherous rake she hardly knew. "But if you insist, you are more than welcome to go with them."

"Why would I choose a boring footman over the company of a delightfully witty young lady?"

Cadence's lips parted. He thought she was delightfully witty?

Focus, she ordered herself sternly. *I'm sure he tells every woman that.*

Except for some reason she had a feeling he didn't. Still...

"It would hardly be proper, Your Grace."

His eyes gleamed. "Funny, the same could be said

about parlors."

"Parlors?" Elsbeth asked, her brow creasing. "What is improper about parlors?"

"Nothing," Cadence said hastily, shooting Colebrook a glare. "Absolutely nothing at all. Parlors are the epitome of propriety."

"That's not what I've heard," he drawled with another suggestive wink that sent heat flooding from the top of her temple all the way down to the tip of her chin. Incorrigible did not even *begin* to describe the Duke of Colebrook!

He was rude, overbearing, irredeemable…suffice it to say, the man was quite beastly.

And he kissed like the devil himself.

Her blush deepening, Cadence looked away. "I'm afraid it is simply out of the question."

"Then I'm afraid you will not get your Christmas tree."

Her incensed gaze flew back to his. "Is this some sort of – of *negotiating* tactic?"

"That depends." He crossed his arms and rocked back on his heels. "Is it working?"

"The servants will talk." Servants *always* talked. And even though her reputation was low, it could always sink lower. Something to remind herself of whenever her resolve began to weaken. Much like it was doing now.

"Oh, I don't think they will." Colebrook gave the careless shrug of a man who had never lost a second's sleep over what others said about him. "What do you think, Elsbeth?"

"About what?" the German maid said innocently. "Miss Fairchild has been in her bedchamber all day. She couldn't possibly have gone on a sleigh ride."

Outnumbered and out of excuses, Cadence bit the inside of her cheek again. Hard. "Fine," she said through gritted teeth. "I'll do it. But only because I need that tree, and only *if* you agree to go straight there and come straight back."

Colebrook grinned. "I'll get your cloak."

THE SLEIGH'S RUNNERS cut effortlessly across the top of the snow as they made their way across an open field. As far as the eye could see everything was a brilliant, sparkling white topped with a clear, vibrant blue. But Justin wasn't looking at the land or the sky. He was looking at Cadence and even though she was pretending not to, she was looking back.

"Will you stop that?" she said finally, twisting in her seat to glare at him. An emerald green hood trimmed with white fur framed her face. Her cheeks were rosy from the cold, her lips red from the wind, her eyes sparkling from thinly veiled annoyance. She was angry with him, and he couldn't blame her. Not when he'd coerced her so shamelessly into joining him. But he wasn't sorry for it, as he had been trying for nigh on a week to get her alone and she'd managed to evade him at every turn. Vexing, quarrelsome woman that she was.

He would have been well served to forget about her. To leave her and Wycliffe Manor all together. He'd need both hands to count the number of women in London who would have eagerly done whatever lascivious act he asked of them, and yet here he was one fixated on the one chit who didn't want anything to do with him.

It didn't make any bloody sense.

Nothing about Miss Cadence Fairchild did.

Maybe that was why he was so intrigued by her.

"Stop what?" He tugged gently on the left trace, guiding the matching team of heavyset bay geldings towards an opening in the trees. Going to the right would have been quicker, but he was enjoying his time with Cadence and he wanted it to last as long as possible.

Even though he was fairly certain if she'd been in possession of a knife she would have already stabbed him in the thigh with it.

"Staring at me as if I were a particularly scrumptious Shrewsbury biscuit."

He lifted a brow. "Do not be ridiculous. Shrewsbury biscuits are terribly bland. I'd rather eat chalk. No, Miss

Fairchild, if you were a dessert you'd be a…Tortuga Rum cake."

"A Tortuga *Rum* cake?"

"Indeed. Sweet and spicy. My two favorite things."

She pursed her lips. "If you were a dessert you'd be rice pudding. Predictable and quick to sour."

Vexing, quarrelsome woman indeed.

"Do you really find me predictable, Miss Fairchild?" They'd entered the woods on a trail only slightly wider than the sleigh. Tiny silver bells attached to the horse's harnesses rang out as the bays trotted on, happy to stretch their legs in the freshly fallen snow.

"Exceedingly so."

"And how is that?" he queried, genuinely curious to know the answer.

"You are not the first rake I have encountered, Your Grace. All of you are the same. You desire what you cannot have, and once you have it, you no longer desire it." She stole a sideways glance at him beneath her lashes. "As I said, predictable and quick to sour."

"And yet you still kissed me," he pointed out.

"A mistake that will not happen again."

"Because I am predictable." Transferring the reins to one hand, he moved the other beneath the heavy blanket covering her from the waist down and ran a single fingertip along the outside of her leg. Her breath catching, she went still as a hare caught out in the open by a hungry fox. He waited for her to tell him to stop, to remove his hand, to bugger off (all of which he would have done, albeit reluctantly) but she remained silent, caught somewhere between denial and desire.

"What was the second bit?" he asked huskily.

"Q-quick to sour," she stammered.

"That's right." He shifted closer to her as his finger slipped between her warm thighs. He began to stroke her through her gown and undergarments; long, slow, lazy passes of his thumb and pointer finger that had her quivering with unspoken need. "Quick to sour." His head canted. "Do you find me sour now, Miss Fairchild?"

Dazed blue eyes met his. "E-exceedingly so," she whispered.

"That's too bad." He watched those expressive eyes darken as he coaxed her slowly but surely towards release. Watched her tongue slide across her bottom lip. Watched her jaw tighten as he held her, held, her held her on the brink…and then sent her tumbling over the other side into blissful oblivion.

Cadence cried out, her hips lifting off the seat as pleasure coursed through her trembling body. To Justin's surprise he felt an answering surge of pleasure in his own loins even though his cock remained untouched and his bollocks heavy and aching.

He'd had never considered himself a selfish lover, but he had always seen to it that his carnal needs were met. Yet as he watched Cadence float down from the high he had sent her soaring towards with a few expert strokes of his fingers he couldn't have felt more satisfied than if he'd experienced his own release.

Curious, that.

Very curious indeed.

"I apologize for being so predictable," he said as she lifted her stunned gaze to his. "I shall endeavor to be more arbitrary in the future." And sliding his hand out from between her thighs he took the reins, clucked his tongue, and set the horses into a canter.

CHAPTER EIGHT

"WHAT DO YOU MEAN, you haven't got an axe?" Standing in the middle of a snow covered lawn with her hands on her hips, Cadence stared at Colebrook in disbelief. They'd come all this way and the great big lummox had forgotten the one thing they needed to chop down the tree! "Unbelievable," she muttered, stuffing her hands into the fur muff stitched to the front of her cloak. "Completely unbelievable."

Colebrook shrugged. "I thought you were bringing one."

"You thought *I* was bringing the axe?" she said incredulously. "And where did you think I was hiding it? Underneath my skirts?"

"I think I would have felt it there, don't you?"

Her mouth opened. Closed. Without another word she

turned on her heel and started back towards the horses. Chuckling under his breath, Colebrook caught up with her before she'd taken more than half a dozen steps.

"Retreating doesn't become you, Miss Fairchild."

"I am not retreating," she corrected him haughtily. "I am returning to the sleigh. It is cold, and since you neglected to bring the axe–"

"You were the one who wanted to commit tree murder." The corners of his mouth twitched. "I presumed you had the weapon handy."

"Tree murder," she repeated. "Of all the ridiculous, absurd–"

"I don't believe the tree thinks it's absurd. Don't worry old chap," he called out cheerfully to the enormous pine towering behind them. "You live to grow another day. I won't let her hurt you.'

Not knowing whether to laugh or throw up her hands, Cadence did a little of both. How could this man – this infuriating, obnoxious, magnificent man – make her purr with passion one second and want to rip out her hair the next? He reminded her of a young boy pulling the braids of a girl he fancied. A young boy who had grown into a charming rake with a heart of – well, not gold. He was far too naughty to have a heart of gold. But not so naughty and irredeemable that it shone copper.

A tarnished silver, she decided. One that would gleam

with a bit of hard work and polish.

Pity she wasn't a maid.

It was rather odd, Cadence reflected, how much her feelings towards men and marriage had changed over the past few weeks. She'd been willing to marry Lord Benfield not because of any strong emotional attachment, but because of his title and social standing and the life he could have given her. A difficult thing to admit, but it was the truth. And not an uncommon one. Love matches were all but unheard of in the *ton*. Marriages of convenience, on the other hand…well, those were a dime a dozen.

Then Lord Benfield had broken her heart, or so she thought, and she went running to her sister…only to discover what a marriage of *in*convenience looked like.

Hannah and Evan's union was not perfect. The Duke of Wycliffe was a difficult man with a difficult past. But even on their worst day it was clear they were genuinely happy. Not just happy, they were in love. And having seen the glow in their eyes when they looked at one another, that was what *she* wanted. Not a marriage of convenience to a boring earl with a button collection, but one comprised and built on love. True love. The sort of love that sonnets were spun from and poets wrote about. The sort of love she would never find with a rogue like Colebrook. No matter how well he kissed or how wicked his fingers.

Which were very, *very* wicked.

In the most delicious way possible.

But lust was not love, and while it was clear Colebrook desired her, Cadence feared that was as far as his feelings went. As far as they'd ever go.

He did not believe in marriage. He'd said as much himself. She was just a shiny new toy he wanted to play with, and once he did he'd grow weary of her and set her back on the shelf like he'd done with the dozens of women before her. Then she would know what *real* heartbreak was like, for she already felt more for Colebrook than she ever had for Benfield. Even though she'd rather burn her second favorite pair of gloves then tell him as much.

"I would like to return now," she announced. "I shall send the footmen back before it gets completely dark. *With* an axe. Then they can – where are you going?"

"There's something I need from inside," Colebrook called back over his shoulder as he trudged through the snow towards his manor. The wind had blown a tall bank up against the front door, forcing him to use a servant's entrance around the side. More snow began to fall lightly from the dull, grey sky as he reached the door and gave it a hard yank. Then another. Finally, on the third pull, the door sprang open.

"Are you coming?" Colebrook shouted, cupping his hands around his mouth so his voice carried clearly across the lawn.

"In *there*?" Cadence eyed the manor dubiously. Without a single candle shining in the windows, the old, dilapidated estate looked nothing short of haunted. She could see where work had been started, but the vast majority of the house was still in need of complete restoration. It would be a stunning showpiece of old architecture mixed with new when it was finished and she would have vastly preferred to wait until then to see the inside of it, but given the choice between remaining outside by herself as darkness slowly descended or accompanying Colebrook within, she was inclined to choose the latter.

"Just couldn't stay away from me, could you?" he said with a grin when she joined him at the door. Out of breath from struggling through the knee-high snow, Cadence could only manage a narrow-eyed glare. His grin broadening, Colebrook gestured her inside. "After you, Miss Fairchild."

She swept past him into a small, unadorned hallway and then waited, shivering, for him to light a candle. "Why on earth wouldn't you leave behind a skeleton staff to tend the estate? Or at least hire a groundskeeper to shovel the pathways."

"Because I didn't plan on coming back here until spring." He held the candle up and she unconsciously leaned towards it, not realizing just how cold she was until the tiny orange flame warmed her icy cheeks. Colebrook frowned. "Poor love. You're half frozen. Here, take my coat and I'll start a fire."

"That really won't be necessary," she protested, but he'd already swept off his greatcoat and draped it over her shoulders like a cloak. It smelled of him, and even though she knew she shouldn't – even though she knew it was just asking for trouble – Cadence hugged the warm garment close to her body and greedily inhaled his woodsy scent.

They passed through the kitchens and down another hallway before entering what she could only assume was the library even though the floor to ceiling shelves had been stripped of books.

"I had them taken to my estate in Colchester," Colebrook remarked when he noted the direction of her gaze. "There aren't many looters this far north, but you never know. Do you like reading, Miss Fairchild?"

"If the most recent addition of *Ackermann's Repository* counts as reading then yes, I enjoy it immensely," she replied honestly. "Hannah's always been the bookworm of the family."

"And what does that make you?" Kneeling in front of

the library's massive stone fireplace, Colebrook began pulling logs from a large metal tin and stacking them in the middle of the hearth while Cadence observed from a few feet back.

"I am afraid I do not know what you mean." Pulling off her hat which was beginning to grow damp from the melting snow that had accumulated on the brim, she tossed it onto a nearby chair and drew Colebrook's coat up to her neck.

"If your sister is the bookworm, who are you?"

"I…I don't know." A line appeared between her brows as she mulled the question over. A month ago she would have answered it easily. *Who am I? I am the future Countess of Benfield.* Except that wasn't really who she *was*, was it? A woman's husband did not define her. Neither did their wealth or the number of shoes in their wardrobe. She used to think those things made a person who they were, but now she knew it was something more. Something that couldn't be bought or acquired. Something that could only come from within.

"That's all right." Throwing the last log into the hearth, Colebrook stood up and brushed his hands off on his trousers. "I don't know who I am either."

Cadence blinked in surprise. "You're a duke."

A duke who looks like an angel and kisses like the devil.

A duke who teases me mercilessly one second and gives me his coat the next.

A duke I am starting to fall helplessly, hopelessly, miserably in love with.

Starting? Her lips twisted in a wry smile. She was nearly halfway there. Despite her attempts to stay away from him, despite her best efforts to forget their kiss, despite knowing it could only end in disaster, she was still falling in love with him. How could she not? He undoubtedly had his faults (lots and lots and *lots* of faults) but she was beginning to suspect there was more to him than what he chose to reveal on the surface.

There was kindness in him. Genuine humor as well, not just the biting remarks he used like a sharp sword to defend himself. Although she still didn't have the slightest idea what exactly he was trying to defend himself against. By all accounts he lived a life of great luxury. One that common men only dreamed about. Anything he wanted he could have with just a snap of his fingers. But perhaps that was part of the problem. When you could have anything you wanted, what did you ask for?

"Aye, I am a duke." He ran a hand through his hair. Like Cadence, he'd discarded his hat and his blond locks gleamed like gold in the flickering candlelight. "And a rake and a scoundrel and a ne'er-do-well, if the rumors can be believed."

"I can believe them," she said dryly.

"And yet here you stand."

"Are you trying to scare me off, Your Grace?"

"Are you frightened?"

"Of you?" She lifted her chin. "Not the least little bit."

Something flickered in his gaze. It was there and gone again too quickly for her to see what it was, but she was left with the distinct impression that it had been something meaningful. Something important. Something that showed Colebrook was more than just a rake and a scoundrel and a ne'er-do-well.

Much more.

"The fire's ready," he said, abruptly changing the subject. Cadence regarded the cold, dark hearth with a lifted brow.

"Don't you need the tinderbox?"

"Right." He rubbed his chin. "The tinderbox."

Her second brow rose to join the first. "You *have* started a fire before, haven't you?"

"Of course. I…just don't know where the servants keep the tinderbox, that's all."

"Here." Striding past him, she stood on her toes and blindly searched the top of the mantle. When her fingers encountered an oval shaped metal box she tossed it to Colebrook, who snatched the tinderbox effortlessly out of the air. "It is almost always kept up here. Makes it easy to find."

"I knew that," he said, although his blank look as he flipped up the lid of the tinderbox and studied its contents had her hiding a smile behind her hand.

Nestled atop a square of scorched linen was everything one would need to create a fire, including a steel striker, flint, and a spunk dipped in brimstone which was used to transfer the flame from linen to logs. Cadence had never started a fire herself, but she'd seen the maids do it enough times to understand how it was done. Colebrook, on the other hand, appeared positively mystified. Not surprising, given that dukes were hardly in a position to tend their own fireplaces. Still, it was rather humorous to realize she knew how to do something he did not.

"I can help you," she offered.

Colebrook scowled. "I said I've started a fire before and I can damn well start this one."

"All right." Holding her hands up, palms facing outwards, she retreated to a large leather armchair. "I'll just be over here. Slowly freezing to death," she muttered under her breath.

"I heard that."

"You were supposed to." Resting her elbow on the edge of the chair and propping her chin in the cusp of her hand, she watched, with no small degree of amusement, as Colebrook tried – and miserably failed – to get the linen to ignite.

Finally, after his fifth attempt yielded nothing more than a tiny spark that immediately went out, he turned to her in exasperation and growled, "The bloody thing's broken."

"Here." Lips twitching as she struggled not to giggle, she stood up and held out her hand. "Let me see the striker and flint. You hold the box. The trick," she said as they stood shoulder to shoulder with their heads bent together, "is to angle the flint just…like…ah!" Triumph shot through her voice as a bright orange spark flew off the edge of the flint and landed on the scorched linen. Within seconds a large flame began to greedily consume the cloth and Colebrook, eyes wide, threw everything – tinderbox and all – into the hearth.

"Wait!" she cried. "That is not what you – oh, never mind. It's too late now. Next time, you needn't toss the entire thing in. Just use the brimstone stick." Laughing, she lifted her gaze to Colebrook's…and her laughter slowly faded away when she saw the heat in his eyes.

"You started the fire," he said huskily, and as he slipped his arm around her waist and drew her against his chest Cadence was left with the distinct impression that he wasn't referring to the logs burning in the hearth.

"Well done, Miss Fairchild."

"It really wasn't that d-difficult," she gasped when he bent his head and traced the sensitive shell of her earlobe with his tongue. "Anyone could have d-done it." Her toes curled inside of her boots. "Well, anyone but a duke a-apparently."

Oh, that felt *heavenly*. Who knew the ear was such a source of untapped pleasure?

The Duke of Colebrook, she thought dazedly as he began to nibble his way down the curve of her neck. *That's who*.

"Are you mocking me?" he asked, lifting his head to stare down at her, blue eyes gleaming.

"Yes," she replied without hesitation. And then, because it seemed the duke's devilishness was contagious, she peered coyly up at him beneath her lashes and said, "What are you going to do about it?"

Chapter Nine

THE FIRE IN THE HEARTH was roaring, but it was nothing compared to the flames that burned between Cadence and Colebrook. She didn't know who kissed whom; only that one moment they were two separate entities and the next they were one being, their lips locked and their hands desperately sliding beneath heavy layers of clothing to touch and stroke and pet.

The coat he'd draped over her shoulders fell away and then so did her dress, leaving her silhouetted against the glow of fire in nothing more than her chemise and petticoat. Trimmed in white satin ribbon the light, airy garments followed the natural curves of her body and Colebrook's eyes took on a hungry, predatory light that sent heat shooting straight down to her loins as he stepped back to admire her.

"*Beautiful.*" He whispered the word as if he were

saying a prayer. Cadence could have easily said the same.

The duke stood before her in just his shirt and trousers. He exuded raw masculinity with every breath, and with his tousled hair and the shadow of whiskers across his chin and jaw it was easy to envision him as a thief or a highwayman or – her blood quickened – a pirate ready to swoop aboard a captured ship and claim what he desired.

Her.

The fantasy only grew when he took grabbed her hip with one hand, slid the other beneath her coiffure, and kissed her with a fervent passion that left her dazed and aching for more. Hair pins scattered across the floor and her mane came tumbling down in a waterfall of ebony silk as the kiss intensified before he wrenched himself free, sculpted chest rising and falling with the force of his breaths.

"We shouldn't," he rasped. "You're an innocent."

She saw the unspoken question in his eyes and knew he was asking her permission to continue. Embracing the wickedness inside of her, she gave it.

"Not after tonight," she whispered, and her belly quivered when his gaze darkened. Yanking a plush fur rug off the back of a sofa, he threw it down in front of the hearth.

"Lift your hands above your head," he said huskily and she obeyed the command without question, any self-consciousness she might have felt drowned out by the overpowering sense of need that throbbed inside of her. When she was dressed in nothing but firelight he took her back into his arms, touching her naked skin with a soft reverence that brought tears to her eyes and wonder to her heart.

He lowered her slowly onto the fur. Pausing only to whisk off his shirt and trousers with an urgency that had her biting back a smile, he followed her down until she was facing him and he was facing her, their naked bodies bathed in shadow and flame, their eyes only for each other.

"Are you certain?" he asked, reaching out to tuck a loose curl behind her ear. Like a flower denied the sun she leaned into his touch, and knew she'd never been as certain of anything else in her entire life.

"Yes," she said simply.

Stretched out on his side he looked as regal as a lion and she was only too happy to play the part of his lioness. Purring when he took her nipple into his mouth, she arched her spine, fingers clutching the rug as his hand slipped between her damp thighs to touch and tease.

Growing bolder, she began to explore his body as he explored hers, her fingertips venturing down over his broad chest and flat stomach. A trail of wiry curls led her to his pulsing arousal. Not knowing what to do, but instinctively wanting to bring him the same pleasure he was bringing her, she encircled his member and began to run her hand from damp tip to turgid base.

"Bloody *hell*," he hissed and she stopped, fearing she'd hurt him, but the sheer ecstasy on his face revealed he was feeling anything but pain.

They continued to stroke one another, sometimes kissing, sometimes not. Cadence lost track of the time. Of their surroundings. Of the fire. There was only Colebrook and the sensations he was wrenching from her with every delicious flick of his finger.

The burst of heat and color came upon her unexpectedly, just as it had done in the sleigh. She cried out, lifting her hips towards Colebrook's hand as her thighs fell open and her head fell back, blue eyes glassy with desire.

He coaxed her back down to earth, whispering naughty words in her ear that both appalled and aroused. She felt the weight of his body as he settled on top of her, and then a different sort of weight between her thighs. Wet and willing she received him easily. There was no pain. No sharp sting she'd been warned about. Only a sense of stretching and fullness, a mild twinge of discomfort as her body grew accustomed to his wide girth, and then nothing but pleasure.

IF HEAVEN WASN'T between Cadence's soft white thighs, Justin didn't want to go.

Sweat glistened on his skin as he held himself back, the muscles in his back clenching and tightening as he tried to hold his orgasm at bay. If he could have made the moment last forever he would have, but her little heels pressing into his flanks wasn't helping his restraint, nor were the tiny mewling sounds she made whenever he rocked so deeply inside of her he could *feel* her clenching around him.

The sensation was nothing short of a bloody miracle and Justin, who had never been particularly religious, clenched his eyes shut and swore he saw Jesus as he thrust himself into Cadence's hot, tight sheath one final time before withdrawing to spill his seed onto the floor.

"Bloody *hell* woman," he groaned, rolling off her and onto his back to stare blindly up at the ceiling. "You've ruined me."

Her hair tickled his chest as she tucked an arm across her breasts and then leaned up on her elbow. Blue eyes sleepy and sated, she gazed down at him, a decidedly feline smile curling one side of her mouth. "How ironic. I was about to say the same thing to you."

Guilt struck him like a fist to the stomach. "Cadence, I–"

"No," she interrupted, shaking her head. "Whatever

you are about to say, I do not want to hear it. This was my decision as much as it was yours. I am a woman full grown, not a naïve debutante in her first Season. I knew what I was doing."

His eyes gleamed. "You can say that again."

She squealed when he picked her up and placed her on top of him. Squealed again when she felt his hard rod nudge at her entrance. And then for a long while the only sounds she made were soft sighs, low moans, and the occasional gasp.

When their second round of lovemaking was over they drowsed in front of the fire until the flames began to a burn a deep, dark red and the air started to cool. Justin helped Cadence back into her gown and then dressed himself, sitting down to pull on his Hessians.

"Ready to return?" he asked, his gaze following her to the window. She stood with her back to him as she watched the falling snow. Her slender body was silhouetted in moonlight, her hair dipped in silver, her skin glowing like a pearl. She was an absolute vision, the most gorgeous woman he had ever laid his eyes upon, and this time when Justin felt a pang deep down inside of his chest he didn't try to stop the screw from loosening. For once he let it turn…and for the first time in a very, very long time the tiny battered box where he kept all of his carefully guarded emotions cracked open…and light spilled out.

"Yes." She turned to face him, then frowned. "But you've forgotten one of your boots."

"What?" he said blankly.

"You only have one boot on," she said, pointing at his feet.

"Right." Feeling as if he'd just awoken from a long dream, Justin sluggishly pulled on his other Hessian, stood up, and held out his arm. "Shall we?"

The floorboards creaked beneath Cadence's boots as she crossed the room and slipped her hand through the crook of his elbow. Her gloved fingers curled familiarly around his bicep as if they'd been there a thousand times before. As if they belonged together. Had always belonged together. Would always belong together.

"Wait," she said, stopping suddenly. "What about the thing you came in here to get?"

Justin glanced down at her upturned face. At her thick lashes and her bright blue eyes and her red lips, swollen from his kisses. At her narrow chin, always tilted in such a way that leaned towards stubbornness. At her lovely neck, the ivory skin gently chafed from his beard. And there was only one answer he could think to give.

"I already have it."

CHAPTER TEN

CHRISTMAS CAME AND WENT. The snow came and stayed. And with every cold day that passed, Cadence fell more in love with the Duke of Colebrook.

He'd asked her to use his given name. Calling him Justin felt both wrong and right at the same time, like when she'd bought an ermine-lined cloak she knew her father couldn't afford...but after she rubbed the soft fur against her cheek she'd been unable to leave the store without it.

He had taken to calling her Cat, a nickname he seemed to particularly enjoy after she shared her dislike for the whiskered creatures. But she couldn't complain. Not when he whispered it in her ear as he slid inside of her.

Cat, you feel so good.

Cat, you're so bloody tight.

Cat, I feel you clenching around me.

Now all he had to do was *say* the word and her nipples hardened, her thighs quivered, and she grew damp in anticipation. Which wasn't a problem when they were in his bedchamber, but when she was trying to take her afternoon tea in the drawing room…well, suffice it to say she'd never be able to look Elsbeth in the eye without blushing ever again.

Justin was naughty and incorrigible; a scoundrel through and through. Their affair hadn't changed that. If anything, he'd become even *more* wicked. And yet she loved every inch of him, naughty bits and all.

She still hadn't told him about her feelings. Honestly, she didn't know if she ever would. If she ever *could.* Their affair was purely physical, and she didn't want to ruin what they had by bringing up what they did not. If she'd been ready to enter a marriage *without* love, then surely she could handle being in an affair *with* love.

Or so she told herself.

"There you are." Sauntering into the parlor where Cadence was reading an outdated edition of *Ackerman's Repository* in front of the fireplace, Justin placed an absent kiss on the top of her head that made her heart ache in a very complicated way. "I've been looking for you all morning."

"I haven't left this room since breakfast." Noting the

way his hair was flattened on one side, she set her reading material aside and rolled her eyes. "Have you been asleep *all* this time?"

"No," he said, scratching his jaw where a full beard had started to grow. It was completely out of fashion, but Cadence loved the way it felt against her…well, suffice it to say she loved the way it felt *everywhere*.

"You have a line on your face from the pillowcase," she pointed out.

"Oh alright," he grumbled. "But it's not my fault I needed some extra sleep. If you hadn't woken me up at half past one in the morning–"

"If memory serves, *you* woke me *up*," she reminded him.

"Aye," he smirked. "And aren't you glad I did?"

Cadence shot a quick glance at the door. She knew the servants were aware of their affair. Servants were always aware of everything. But there was a difference between forgetting her nightdress in Justin's chambers and speaking about their lovemaking out loud where anyone could overhear.

"What have I said about discussing bedroom matters outside of the bedroom?" she hissed.

"That it's an excellent topic of conversation?" Sitting on the armrest of her chair, he reached behind her and started to massage her shoulders. She swatted his hands away.

"You know, I think you do it on purpose."

"Do what on purpose?"

"Irritate me."

His brows gathered. "Well of course I do it on purpose. It'd be no fun otherwise. Speaking of fun, you need to get dressed for outside."

Cadence looked at the door again to ensure no one was listening before she batted her lashes and said, "I think that's the first time you've ever told me to put on *more* clothes."

The duke wasn't the only one who could tease. Since their visit to Colebrook Manor she'd become increasingly comfortable with the side of herself she'd always had to hide from Lord Benfield. The side that wasn't always polished or polite or ladylike. The side that kissed dukes in drawing rooms. And parlors. And libraries. And, on at least one memorable occasion, the first floor linen closet.

"You're right," he frowned. "I am probably ill. Here, feel my temple."

"Get *off*," she giggled when he all but collapsed into her arms. After stealing a quick kiss, he bounded to his feet.

"Come along, then. We've snow angels to make."

"*Snow angels*?" she repeated, certain she'd misheard him. "Those are for children."

"Says someone who is afraid their snow angel is going to pale in comparison to mine."

She pursed her lips. "Is that a challenge?"

"We can make it one." His teeth flashed in a grin. "The winner gets to claim a prize."

"Anything they want?"

"Anything."

Love me as I love you.

The thought, unbidden and unwanted, caused the color to leech from Cadence's cheeks.

Love wasn't something that could be won in a contest. It couldn't be asked for or demanded. It had to be freely given, and she desperately feared it was the one gift her duke, as rich as he was, would never be able to afford to give her.

Which is fine, her head argued. *Positively fine. Everything is fine.*

She waited for her heart's rebuttal, but for once it was uncharacteristically silent.

"Cat?" said Justin, his grin fading as he studied her. "Is something the matter?"

"No." Forcing her lips to form something that vaguely resembled a smile, she patted his chest. "Nothing is the matter. Nothing at all. Let's go make snow angels."

SOMETHING WAS THE MATTER. Justin could feel it. Hell,

the entire bloody household could feel it. But no matter how many different times or how many different ways he asked, Cadence always gave him the same answer: *I'm fine. Everything is fine. You are being foolish.*

He may have been foolish, but even he knew that when a woman said 'everything is fine' what she *really* meant was 'everything is awful and if you don't find out what's bothering me soon you're going to be miserable for the rest of your natural born life'.

Since he wasn't a man who particularly enjoyed misery, he was determined to find out what was bothering his sad-eyed Cat. Unfortunately, matters weren't helped by the fact that, for the most part, she was still acting the same as she ever had.

Inside his bedchamber she was playful and passionate. Outside of it she was vexing and vivacious. But every once in a while he'd happen to glance at her when she didn't know he was looking and the sadness in those crystal blue eyes would take his breath away.

Deep down inside Justin knew what the problem was. A part of him had always known, because he knew Cadence. They may have only met a short time ago, but he already knew her like he knew himself. And because he knew her so well, he knew what she wanted. What she needed. What she was afraid to ask for and he was equally afraid to give.

Love.

It always came down to love.

If not for Jessica and the scars she'd left behind, Justin had no doubt he would have already pledged his heart to Cadence. Because he *did* love her. How could he not? She was everything he'd always wanted and everything he'd never known he needed.

She challenged him. Angered him. Made him want to curse one second and kiss her breathless the next. She wasn't afraid of him. More than that, she wasn't impressed by him. And that made all the difference in the world.

He could be himself around her. Could let his armored shield of sarcasm and cynicism fall away to reveal the man behind the mask. The man he'd been before Jessica came along and showed him how truly vicious and deceptive women could be. The man he'd been before he shoved all his feelings away in that damn box.

Jessica's deception still angered him; more so now than ever before because he knew that what he'd felt for her hadn't been love. Lust? Most certainly. Infatuation? Definitely. But love? No. Whatever they'd had between them…it hadn't been love. He could see that now. As clearly as he'd ever seen anything.

Love did not manipulate. It did not make bargains. It did not lie.

Love was having your sanity questioned by a pint-sized mermaid with hair the color of a raven's wing and eyes that sparkled like stars. Love was having your entire world upended by a single kiss. Love was going out to cut down a tree and forgetting the bloody axe because it was never about the tree. It was always about her. It was always going to be about her. It was always *meant* to be about her.

And it was past time he bloody well told her so.

"Are you awake, Cat?" Sitting up in the bed they'd shared every night since the library, Justin gently stroked a fingertip down the length of her bare arm. Underneath the coverlet she wore only a thin white shift, the hem of which had ridden up while she slept curled against him, exposing a plump creamy thigh for his viewing pleasure.

God, she was beautiful. Not just on the outside, as Jessica had been, but on the inside as well. She wasn't perfect – neither of them were – but it was her flaws that endeared her to him the most. She was perfectly imperfect, and as he gazed down at her he was filled with so much love he ached.

"What time is it?" she murmured sleepily.

"Time to wake up." Lowering his head, he started to nibble her ear until her eyes flew open and she shot upright, the top of her head connecting with the bottom of his nose in an unexpected blow that sent him reeling.

"Bloody hell woman," he complained, running a finger under his nostrils to check for blood. "A little warning next time."

"What is it?" she asked in a panicked voice. "What's wrong? Have my sister and Wycliffe returned?" Flipping around, she sat up on her knees and tried to peer out the window. Heaving an exaggerated sigh, Justin wrapped his arms around her and hauled her back to the middle of the bed.

"Nothing is wrong," he murmured against her hair. "I've simply something I would like to tell you."

"Oh." Relaxing, she let her head fall against his chest. "I thought that since you were awake before noon the sky was falling down on us."

Justin scowled. "I don't sleep *that* much."

Twisting in his arms, she regarded him with an arched brow. "You're like an overfed cat languishing on a windowsill. All you do is sleep."

"That's as insulting to me as it is cats."

Cadence lifted her shoulder in an elegant shrug. "Sometimes the truth hurts."

It wasn't exactly the romantic opening he'd been hoping for, but it was better than nothing. He cleared his throat. "Speaking of which, there's something I—"

"Did you hear that?" Fighting her way out of his embrace, she went back to her knees and pressed her face against the frosted glass window pane. Whatever she saw immediately caused her entire body to freeze. "Oh no," she whispered. "No, no, no."

"What?" Justin demanded. "What is it?"

"Wycliffe's carriage. It's in the drive."

The tension that had started to rise within him immediately subsided. "Is that all? Well, we knew they'd return sooner or later."

"Yes." Worrying her bottom lip between her teeth, she slid back beneath the covers. "But I was hoping it would be later instead of sooner. What if they come in here and see us?"

"Come into my private chambers?" he scoffed. "Wycliffe wouldn't dare."

But no more had he spoken aloud than a knock sounded at the door.

CHAPTER ELEVEN

"COLEBROOK? ARE YOU IN HERE? My wife is looking for her sister and – *what the devil is going on*?" Wycliffe roared when he opened the door all the way and saw Cadence and Justin in bed together.

Grabbing the edge of the blanket, Cadence yanked it up to her chin and pinched her eyes shut, desperately wishing she was in the midst of a nightmare and Hannah and Wycliffe weren't standing there staring at her with shock on their faces.

"Yes," Hannah piped up from beside her husband. "What *is* going on here?"

Cadence winced. Not a nightmare, then.

Drats.

Her cheeks as red as the holly berries decorating the

window sills, she peeked sideways at Justin. He, of course, did not look the least bit embarrassed. If anything, he appeared amused.

"What does it look like, old chap?" Curving his arm around Cadence's shoulders, he drew her protectively against his side and kissed her temple. "Just count yourself lucky you didn't pop in five minutes later. Then you really would have – ouch," he complained when she kicked him underneath the covers. "What was that for?"

"They don't need details," she hissed, beyond mortified.

"They did ask," he said mildly.

"You really are incorrigible!" And she was a fool – a *fool!* – for having fallen in love with him. Now there was nothing to do about it but face the music. Or, in this case, the looming disapproval of her sister and brother-in-law.

Truth be told, she'd always known this day was coming. She'd known it from the moment she and Justin made love for the first time. She just hadn't been expecting it quite so soon.

The end, she thought as a heavy ache settled in her chest and tears threatened the corners of her eyes. They were already at the end and she'd hardly had any time to enjoy the beginning.

But maybe it is better this way, she told herself even as Justin reached for her hand beneath the covers and squeezed her fingers tight. She was ruined, of course. Completely and utterly ruined. But there was always a steep price to pay when one dared dance too close to the sun, and even though her wings were burned beyond measure it had been worth it. *He* had been worth it.

And I will not apologize, she thought, steeling herself against the shame that threatened. *I followed my heart and I have nothing to be sorry for.*

Except for the number of cats I'm going to own.

"How long has this been going on?" Wycliffe demanded.

"I believe we started at half past ten last night." Justin rubbed his jaw. "Or was it eleven? I'll admit, I wasn't keeping track of the time. Ah," he grinned when Wycliffe growled. "Do you mean how long I've been having an affair with your delightful sister-in-law? That began a week or so after you left for your honeymoon. How was it, by the way?"

"Very nice," said Hannah. "Thank you for asking. The weather could have been a bit warmer, but given the time of year–"

"You bloody bastard," Wycliffe snarled as he lunged forward. With a surprised squeak his wife grabbed his arm and dragged him back.

"Stop that," she scolded, wagging her finger at him. "This is no time or place for fighting."

"You're right. It's time for pistols. Pick your second, Colebrook."

Cadence exchanged an alarmed glance with her sister.

"Now, now," Hannah said in a low, soothing murmur. "I am certain this can be resolved without violence. What would I do if something happened to you, my darling?"

As if by magic Wycliffe's knotted shoulders relaxed and the glint of murderous rage faded from his eyes. Cadence felt a lump form in her throat when he looked down at his little wife with what could only be described as complete and total adoration. What she wouldn't give to have Justin look at *her* like that. As if she were his entire world, and nothing existed inside of it except for the two of them.

"Nothing is going to happen to me," Wycliffe assured Hannah. Then he looked up at the bed and the corners of his mouth tightened. "But something *is* going to happen to that damned scoundrel. For once, he's going to held responsible for his actions. Get dressed, Colebrook. You've a wedding to attend."

"Oh?" Justin lifted a brow. "And whose wedding is that?"

Wycliffe smiled grimly. "Yours."

"There's really no need for that," said Cadence. Three months ago she would have leapt at the opportunity to become a duchess. Now the thought of forcing Justin into a marriage he didn't want turned her blood cold. "I will be fine."

"You heard the lady," Justin said mildly. "She'll be fine. Now I don't mean to be rude, but could you please get the hell out of my bedchamber?"

"So you can escape out the nearest window?" Wycliffe snarled. "I think not."

"Really," Cadence began, "there's no cause for all–"

"As *tempting* as jumping out the window sounds," Justin interrupted, "I need you to leave so I can tell Miss Fairchild how much I love her."

"–of this dra...*what* did you just say?" Cadence gasped, looking at Justin with wide, startled eyes. He couldn't have just said what she'd thought he'd said.

Could he?

"Oh my," Hannah said, bringing her hands up to her mouth. "I knew it. I just *knew* it."

"You knew what?" Wycliffe asked.

"I knew they were going to fall in love." She elbowed her husband in the ribs. "You'd have known it too if you had a romantic bone in your body."

"I'm romantic," he growled. "Who said I wasn't romantic?"

"Come on. Let's give them some time alone." Taking her husband by the hand, Hannah half led, half dragged him out the door and closed it soundly behind them.

Cadence stared at Justin. Justin stared at Cadence. For a few seconds there was only a heavy, awkward silence and then they both tried to speak at once.

"What do you mean you love–"

"That wasn't the way I wanted to–"

They broke off. Sweeping an agitated hand through his hair, Justin stood up and began to pace back and forth at the foot of the bed, his bare feet sinking silently into the thick rug.

"I'm sorry, Cat. That wasn't the way I wanted to tell you."

"Tell me what?" she whispered.

He stopped short. "That I love you, of course."

"Of course," she repeated faintly.

"I have for quite some time," he continued. "Maybe from the first moment we met, even though you *did* think I was Wycliffe."

"A terrible mistake." She desperately searched his face, looking for some sort of sign that he was joking, or that she was dreaming, but what she saw instead stole the breath from her lungs and brought tears, the happiest of tears, to her eyes.

He was gazing at her as if she was the only woman in the world...and he would never let her go.

"You love me," she said hoarsely. "You really do love me."

Justin stopped and frowned. "I know I do. Did I not make myself – don't cry," he exclaimed in alarm. "Why are you crying?"

"B-because I'm so *happy*," she sniffled as tears rolled down her cheeks.

"Vexing, quarrelsome woman," he said affectionately. Climbing back into bed, he pulled her onto his lap and kissed her neck. "How could I not love you? You're the only one who would ever dare tell me how beastly I am to my face."

She twisted to face him. "You *are* beastly."

"See?" he grinned. "I'd be mad with arrogance without you. Marry me, Cat, and save the *ton* from another conceited, self-entitled duke."

"You're always going to be conceited and self-entitled. I don't think marriage will fix that." She dashed her fingers across her cheeks. Now wasn't the time for tears. It was the time for happiness and celebration. Her duke loved her. He *loved* her. And she loved him back. Madly. Deliriously. Wildly. She loved him with everything that she had. Not because he was a duke, or because he was wealthy. But because he was *him*. And there wasn't a single thing she would change.

"Well?" he asked. "Will you?"

"Will I what?"

"*Marry* me, Cat. Will you marry me or not?"

Her lips twitched. "With a romantic proposal like that, how could I refuse?"

"It's Wycliffe's fault," he scowled. "It *was* going to be romantic until that great big ox came barging in here."

"Why?" she said softly. "Why do you want to marry me now? I thought you didn't believe in marriage."

He was quiet for a long moment. "I didn't. But then I finally opened the box."

Her brow knitted in confusion. "What box?"

"It isn't important. The only thing important is how much I love you." Tilting her chin up, he captured her mouth in a long, slow kiss. "Which is more than I ever thought possible. Marry me, Miss Cadence Fairchild. Make an honest man out of this hopeless rogue."

"All right," she said, her eyes shining. "I'll marry you. But only if you promise to never stop being a rogue."

Justin had her flat on her back and her shift pulled up past her waist before she could blink. "That's a promise I will be happy to keep."

And, much to Cadence's wicked delight, he proceeded to do just that.

EPILOGUE

CADENCE AND JUSTIN were married on the first day of spring. The groom wore black. The bride wore pale blue. From the beginning of the ceremony to the end, they both wore smiles. And they only had eyes for each other.

As the months and years went by, it was clear they weren't the perfect husband and wife. They argued and fought and disagreed. But that was what made their marriage perfectly *im*perfect. And even though there were days when Cadence wanted to toss Justin out the nearest window and he would have loved to throw her in the snow, they always mended their differences because the only thing better than fighting was making up.

On their third anniversary they welcomed a daughter, and then shortly thereafter a son. The children both had their mother's eyes but their father's sense of humor, and before long little Anne and James were driving their parents crazy in the best possible way.

"Do you remember our very first Christmas tree?" Leaning against Justin's hard chest as she watched their children throw snowballs at each other out the window, Cadence tilted her head back and smiled up at him.

My husband, she thought happily. *My wonderful, handsome, roguish husband. How I love you.*

"You mean the one we couldn't cut down because you forgot to bring the axe?" Time had brought a sprinkling of gray to Justin's blond hair, but it had done nothing to dull his sharp wit.

Cadence rolled her eyes. "For the hundredth time, *you* were supposed to bring the axe."

"I don't remember that part."

Of course he didn't.

"What part *do* you remember?" she asked.

"I believe, if memory serves, there was a lot of this." Spinning her around in his arms, he drew her earlobe between his teeth. "And this," he murmured as his hands traveled up to cup her breasts.

"Stop that," she said, swatting half-heartedly at his arm. "The children might see."

"The only thing they'll see is how much their father loves their mother. Besides, James was quite clear what he would like this year for Christmas."

"Oh?" she said, noting the devilish glint in his eye.

"And what's that?"

"A baby brother."

"Justin!" she squealed as he scooped her up in his arms and headed for the stairs.

"Yes?" he said, pausing at the bottom step.

All these years later and she still burned for him as much as she ever had. Looping her arms around his neck, she pressed her lips to his neck. "Hurry."

Made in the USA
Middletown, DE
22 March 2019